Th

When it wa

Cleo and Robb

for the front gates. JP Edsel-Mellon's gold Rolls-Royce was directly in front of the Walton School in the spot where the two buses that transported students to after-school activities usually parked. One of the bus drivers was asking the chauffeur to move the car, but the bearded man only stood there appearing not to hear a word. In a matter of minutes, the two bus drivers were yelling at the limo driver at the top of their lungs.

The chauffeur moved like a marionette soldier as he opened the door, took JP's bag with a stiff arm, then made the slightest of bows as JP entered the backseat. As Carl formally presented the bag to the boy, one book fell out and to the ground. When the shifty-eyed man leaned over to pick up the textbook, his uniform jacket flipped open, exposing a shoulder holster and gun. . . .

The *Undercover Cleo* Series by Anne Scott

UNDERCOVER CLEO
STAGE FRIGHT
THE CANINE CAPER

UNDERCOVER CLEO

The Canine Caper

ANNE SCOTT

BERKLEY BOOKS, NEW YORK

UNDERCOVER CLEO: THE CANINE CAPER

A Berkley Book/published by arrangement with
the author

PRINTING HISTORY
Berkley edition/May 1996

For information address:
The Berkley Publishing Group,
200 Madison Avenue, New York, New York 10016.

ISBN: 0-425-15293-6

BERKLEY®
Berkley Books are published by The Berkley Publishing Group,
200 Madison Avenue, New York, New York 10016.
BERKLEY and the "B" design
are trademarks belonging to Berkley Publishing Corporation.

PRINTED IN THE UNITED STATES OF AMERICA

10 9 8 7 6 5 4 3 2 1

ACKNOWLEDGMENTS

My thanks to the following for their expert advice: Don and Richard at Sam's Camera Exchange in Scarsdale, NY; Ivy Fischer Stone; and especially to Laura Anne Gilman, whose meticulous care and fabulous suggestions make my work look so much better.

Chapter 1

Cleo Oliver was late. Not by much, just five minutes or so, but it was enough to make her take extra-long, extra-quick strides on her way to school. She didn't even notice that the daffodils around the base of the trees on 69th Street were pushing their way out of the ground, or that a red-breasted robin was hopping down the sidewalk. All Cleo knew was that the day had not started out well.

It was one of those mornings when no matter what she'd tried, her thick black hair simply refused to respond. It seemed every strand on her head wanted to go in its own direction and not even barrettes or a headband could control it. She'd had to settle for a baseball cap. Sometimes covering up the problem was the only answer.

On top of having a thoroughly rotten hair day, she'd

planned to wear her green cashmere sweater to school, but when she'd slipped it on, it had been way too small. The sleeves that had once hit the tip of her elbow were now halfway to her armpit, and instead of reaching her waist, the sweater screeched to a halt a good inch above her belly button. Cleo would have considered wearing the beautiful cashmere top as a midriff if she hadn't been so self-conscious about her ribs that, in her mind at least, stuck out like a skeleton's.

With regret, she'd pulled off the sweater, made a note to give it to Nortrud, the housekeeper, to donate to the Salvation Army, and put on a big denim shirt that she knew would fit. Then, feeling like a total grungemeister, the girl had left the apartment and headed toward school.

Cleo Oliver was thirteen and had been growing at an alarming rate for more than two years now. She was five feet nine inches, or she had been last fall anyway. Judging from the fit of her sweater, she calculated that she had sprouted another half inch . . . maybe more.

If anyone calls me "the giraffe" today, thought Cleo, *I'll go over the edge. They'll have to take me away in a straitjacket.* She set her jaw and narrowed her eyes as she neared The Walton School, a private, coed institution on the Upper West Side of Manhattan. Cleo had attended Walton since kindergarten and expected to be there until she graduated from high school. She had quite a few friends there, but lately, since she'd started towering over everyone, she hadn't really felt like she fit in.

She paused for a moment when she got near the historic brick building and watched the crowds of students piling through the iron gates. Cleo resumed her hurried speed toward the small courtyard, until someone looked in her direction, then pointed. To her horror, everyone turned to stare at her.

Great, she thought. *The worst day of my life and I can't even get into school without the whole world noticing*. Then she saw more kids coming out of the building to gape. This was too much.

I can't look that bad, she finally decided. Slowly she turned to look over her shoulder . . . and saw a polished gold limousine driving down the street.

No wonder, thought Cleo as she watched the long car slow down. Though limos were a fairly common sight in New York City, they were usually black or white or occasionally navy-blue. Cleo leaned forward to look at a hood ornament on the front of the car, a small winged figure flying forward. It couldn't be.

"A stretch Rolls-Royce," said Robbi Richards to Cleo as she came up behind her. "Can you believe it? You've got to have mountains of money to drive that monster." The diminutive girl who was Cleo's best friend was so short that she had to stand on tiptoe to reach Cleo's ear. "Come to think of it, I'd also have to say a person would have to have mountains of bad taste, too."

As the limousine pulled to a stop in front of the school, dazzling shafts of sunlight reflecting off of the gold grill made the two girls look away, and they turned and walked side by side into the Walton courtyard.

Cleo and Robbi were the oddest of odd couples. Their most noticeable difference was that, at four feet ten inches, Robbi measured nearly a foot shorter than Cleo. Then there was the fact that Cleo had almost pitch-black hair and snow-white skin, and Robbi, who was half Japanese, had dark reddish-brown hair and olive skin. Even more than the physical differences were the contrasts in personality. While Cleo shied away from loud colors or wild and crazy clothing styles that would call attention to herself, her friend reveled in the outrageous. Still, despite their dissimilar qualities, the two girls had forged a bond that couldn't be any stronger if they had been twins.

"Wow, I must really be late if you're already here," Cleo said, only half joking. While Cleo made an effort to be on time, if not early, for everything, Robbi scooted in to class almost every day at the last possible minute.

The tall teenager checked her watch and saw she still had four minutes before the first bell. She glanced back to the street in time to see a chauffeur getting out of the driver's side door of the limousine.

The slight, devilish-looking man had a pointy beard and wore a uniform complete with cap and an excess of gold trim. As he came around the car, he glanced over at the growing crowd of students with the coldest eyes Cleo had ever seen. Now every student in the

Walton courtyard was dying to get a glimpse of the occupant in the back seat of the gold Rolls-Royce.

The chauffeur opened the door and reached in, withdrawing a leather bag that Cleo recognized as MCM, one of the most expensive makes of luggage. Then the man stood and stepped back to make way for his passenger.

Cleo held her breath, expecting a princess or maybe a president of a South American nation to get out of the car, and she wondered why an important person would be visiting Walton today. She couldn't remember seeing any special guests or assemblies on the school schedule, but maybe this was a surprise visit by a famous former alumnus. After all, The Walton School proudly claimed quite a few politicians and celebrities among their graduates.

"Hey, what's the big deal, everybody?" said Andy Monahan much too loudly. "It's only a kid." Andy was the reigning star of several of Walton's athletic teams, but he wasn't exactly a master of subtlety.

The sandy-haired boy who stepped out of the limo appeared startled as he looked at the group of students watching him, but he gathered his composure almost immediately, and without so much as a sideways glance at the chauffeur, put his hand out palm up. The uniformed man responded by giving the leather bag to the boy.

"That will be all for now, Carl," said the boy. He adjusted his oval-shaped wire-framed glasses, lifted his chin, and strode through the crowd.

Cleo saw that the boy was small, somewhat shorter

than the other boys at Walton, and fairly thin. Given her current growth spurt, height was the number-one thing the tall girl noticed about anyone these days.

"Who do you think this guy is?" said Cleo to Robbi. Though there were a few Walton students from very wealthy families who were driven to school in limos, they opened their own doors and carried their own books. This boy, who looked like a walking ad for Brooks Brothers with his navy-blue blazer, club tie, gray pants, and black loafers, was a different story.

"More importantly," remarked Robbi, "is who does *he* think he is? What a poophead." She turned away and headed into the building, completely turned off by the boy's obvious snobbishness.

Cleo decided it was time to get to class and followed her friend into the school. Both girls scurried up to the fourth floor where the eighth-graders had their lockers. They dropped off some of their books, then headed toward homeroom.

To their surprise, the new boy was in the room, standing next to Mr. Gorgola's desk. Once everyone had taken their seats, the teacher cleared his throat.

"Everybody, I'd like to introduce a new student at Walton. This is Jon Edsel-Mellon. He's going to be joining us for the rest of the year and, we hope, after that as well."

Robbi reached over and jabbed Cleo in the arm. "Edsel-Mellon? No wonder he came in that car." The boy was the son of billionaire entrepreneur and real estate developer Herbert Edsel-Mellon. "They're practically the richest people on the planet."

Cleo nodded her head in appreciation. The family name was always in the news. No matter what Jon's father did, he was always wildly successful. Everyone had heard of the Edsel-Mellons.

The class murmured greetings to the boy, who held up his hand to silence them. "A pleasure, I'm sure," he said, sounding like he didn't mean a bit of it. "Call me JP. My name is Jonathan Packard, and no one"—he let his gaze hit everyone in the room—"calls me Jon."

Cleo and Robbi stifled giggles as they mouthed "JP" to each other. Just then, the bell rang, signaling that it was time to move on to first period.

The two friends had the first couple of classes together and when they got to second period, they found JP sitting in one of the front seats of the class.

"How exciting," said Robbi dryly. " 'Mr. Snoots' is here." She walked up to the boy. "Uh, excuse me, that's my seat."

JP glanced up at Robbi, then looked toward the teacher, Ms. Stathakis, and raised his hand. "Oh, ma'am? Didn't you say I should take any seat? I mean, it is my first day and all."

Ms. Stathakis smiled, which was unusual for the serious teacher. "Robbi, you don't mind, do you? After all, you've been at Walton for years now. This is JP's first day."

Robbi put on a sweet and very fake grin. "Of course I don't mind, Ms. Stathakis. JP's more than welcome to my chair. I'll just take one of the yucky seats in the *back*." English was Robbi's favorite class and she loved her front and center desk.

All during second period, Cleo watched and listened as her friend raised her hand to ask questions, shouting as if she were in the next state, while JP sat up front looking extremely bored. Things got worse when Ms. Stathakis selected two teams for an impromptu debate on the book the class was studying, Charles Dickens's *Great Expectations*.

Cleo hated debating with a passion. She loathed being put on the spot in front of her classmates, and even though she was sure Ms. Stathakis had noticed that fact, it didn't seem to have fazed the teacher in the least. Cleo got assigned to team A.

Robbi Richards, on the other hand, was a debating fanatic and though she raised her hand and waved it like a windup toy gone berserk, she wasn't chosen for either team that morning. Cleo flashed her friend a sympathetic shrug as she trudged toward the front of the room to stand with her fellow teammates, one of whom was JP Edsel-Mellon.

JP showed no sign of wanting to participate whatsoever. His most enthusiastic gesture was to yawn and roll his eyes, which Cleo interpreted as a prelude to disaster. But surprisingly, when the debate started, the boy popped off facts, sharp rebuttals, and answers to almost every remark made to him. He amazed the class with his knowledge and understanding of *Great Expectations*, and due mostly to his input, Cleo's team won the debate.

Immediately after class, the rest of the students disappeared into the hallway, trying to get to their next destination in the allotted three minutes, but Cleo decided to stay behind. She had a study period next and was already carrying her math and history books. Besides, she wanted to congratulate her new classmate for helping win the debate, as well as welcome him to Walton. One of Cleo's friends, Jason Garrett, had told her that when he was new to the school earlier in the year, most of the students had hardly bothered to talk to him at all. Cleo didn't want to be guilty of that crime of omission herself, and she grabbed the back of Robbi's jacket.

"Wait up a sec, Rob," said Cleo. "I just want to say something to JP."

Robbi growled, but waited. Besides, her next class was gym and she could get away with being several minutes late. Cleo looked at JP and seeing again just how short the boy was, she scrunched herself down as best as she could before walking over.

"That was great," she said. "It was amazing how you answered everything like perfectly. We wouldn't have won without your help."

JP let out a huff. "I read *Great Expectations* when I was nine. You know, I thought this was supposed to be a school with educated students, but I can see now that I was thoroughly misinformed." With that, he picked up his book bag and walked off, leaving behind a shocked Cleo and Robbi.

"He just totally dissed the whole school," said Cleo.

Robbi only let out a huff as if to say "I told you so," then pointed after the boy. "And get a load of that."

Despite his cold manner and rude behavior, JP had a flock of admirers following him as he walked to his next class. A moment later a group of cheerleaders came fluttering around the boy, vying for his attention, then several guys on the football team showed up, good-naturedly punching the rich boy's arm. To Cleo, JP seemed to be looking down his nose at all of them.

At lunchtime, Cleo and Robbi were only slightly surprised to see the Edsel-Mellon boy seated at a center table amid many of the most popular kids in Walton.

"Gee," said Robbi, "I guess all it takes is money and you're guaranteed a place at the top."

Cleo nodded and wondered if she would actually feel good being invited to join the popular clique at the center table if the only reason was that her family was rich. She decided that she would be happier sitting in a back corner with her own pals, but it would be nice, just once, to be invited into the popular kids' group. Cleo sighed and followed Robbi to the back table.

When it was, at last, time to go home for the day, Cleo and Robbi banged their lockers shut and headed for the front gates where they ran into a standoff. The gold Rolls-Royce was directly in front of the Walton gates in the spot where the two buses that transported students to after-school activities usually parked. One of the bus drivers was asking the chauffeur to move the car, but the bearded man only stood there appearing not to hear a word. In a matter of minutes the two bus drivers were yelling at the limo driver at the top of their lungs.

It hadn't been a stellar day as far as Cleo was concerned and this annoyed her even more. Both Cleo and Robbi were doing their utmost to tune out the scene, but when they heard the crowd saying their good-byes to JP, they couldn't help glancing back.

The chauffeur moved like a marionette soldier as he opened the door, took the boy's bag with a stiff arm, then made the slightest of bows as JP entered the backseat. As Carl formally presented the bag to the boy, one book fell out and to the ground. From their vantage point, Cleo and Robbi saw something no one else could see. When the shifty-eyed man leaned over to pick up the textbook, his uniform jacket flipped open, exposing a shoulder holster and gun.

Chapter 2

Robbi grabbed Cleo's elbow and yanked hard. Without a word, the two girls hurried away, afraid they might have seen something they shouldn't have.

"Wow," said Cleo once she was sure they were out of earshot of the car. "Do you think that was a real gun?"

Robbi turned to stare at her friend. "Get real. He's probably a bodyguard as well as a chauffeur. Families like the Edsel-Mellons always have kidnapping threats, although you'd think JP's parents would be glad to get rid of him. That guy is a real pain in the"—and she patted her butt as she said—"neck."

Cleo joined Robbi in a laugh as they came to their favorite music store, The Hits. They split up, Robbi going down the escalator of the humongous store to check out the oldies section in the basement, while

Cleo stayed on the main floor to see what was new. After half an hour of looking and listening, Robbi came upstairs with a cassette tape of an obscure British pop group from the seventies. Cleo had never heard of the group, Purple Starshine, but she nodded appreciatively, knowing her friend had a knack for digging out music that almost no one had ever listened to before.

Cleo had found a CD she really liked by a hot, up-and-coming vocalist who went by the single name Tilly, but because the album had just been released, the girl knew it would probably cost a good deal more than the bargain basement oldie that Robbi was holding. One glance at the price tag told Cleo that she'd have to wait until next Sunday when she got her allowance. *How does money go so fast?* she asked herself. It seemed like there was never enough.

With a wistful sigh, Cleo put the CD back on the rack. She went with Robbi as the girl made her purchase, then the two friends went to their respective homes.

The Olivers lived directly across the street from Central Park in a turn-of-the-century co-op building. Their apartment, on the fifteenth floor, was a high-ceilinged, seven-room dwelling that had as much space as a typical house.

"Hi, Terry," said Cleo as she entered the lobby. Terry was one of the five men who rotated in eight-hour shifts to cover the front entrance. The doormen knew every occupant by sight and none of them would dare let an unfamiliar person get past them. As far as Cleo knew, there hadn't been a single crime in the building in years.

"Miss Cleo." Terry touched his hand to his cap and nodded in greeting as the girl went past to the elevator.

It was a relief to come home and finally be able to pull off the baseball cap. Cleo didn't like to wear hats all day, they seemed to make her head ache, and now she reached up and massaged her scalp with both hands. "Hi, Nortrud," she called as she let herself into the apartment.

Nortrud, the Olivers' housekeeper, responded with an operatic, "In the kitchen, dearie."

The girl popped open the swinging door to the kitchen, gave the woman a wave, then scooted into her bedroom. Cleo's room had long ago been the maid's quarters and was only steps from the kitchen. She dropped her books on her desk, a miniature antique rolltop, then sat in her cuddy chair.

The early American wing-backed chair had been in Cleo's mother's family for years and it was here that Cleo, as a little girl, had sat for a "cuddy" with her mother or father. The girl had listened to innumerable stories nestled in the heirloom piece and it was still her favorite place to curl up. She kicked off her shoes and a moment later Phoebe, Cleo's pet mini-lop rabbit, made an appearance from beneath the skirt of the chair.

"Hey, Feeb," said Cleo. Phoebe had started life in the Oliver household as a tiny, two-pound bunny, but had kept growing and growing and growing until she'd reached her current weight of ten pounds. The rabbit was litter box-trained and not only had free run of the Oliver apartment, but sincerely believed that she ruled the entire household.

Cleo hefted the tan beast into her lap and stroked the long floppy ears until Phoebe began making a clucking sound with her teeth, the rabbit equivalent of purring. "Come on, Bun," said the girl, "let's get a snack." She set the animal down and went out to the kitchen with Phoebe trotting along close behind.

Nortrud was scrubbing the walls of the oven. The sturdy-looking woman had been with the Olivers from before Cleo was born and considered it her responsibility not only to take care of household chores, but the people who lived there as well. Since the housekeeper had no family of her own, she doted all the more on the three Olivers and they, in return, adored Nortrud.

"Can't believe how much crud is on the bottom of this oven," said Nortrud. "Your father must have been cooking again." She brushed some of her wiry hair, which she'd recently dyed an odd shade of orangy-red, away from her forehead.

Cleo nodded her head. "Chinese barbecued ribs. They probably would have been really good except he added way too much chili oil."

Nortrud clucked sympathetically. "When is he ever going to learn?"

Cleo made a face and shook her head. "I don't know, but this time even *he* couldn't eat them." On weekends Mr. Oliver loved to experiment in the kitchen, invariably leaving some kind of major mess for the housekeeper to deal with on Monday morning.

Nortrud stood up and rubbed the small of her back. "Shall I fix you a snack, dearie?"

"No thanks," said Cleo. "I think I'll just have a banana." She grabbed a piece of fruit from the basket on the kitchen table, peeled it, then broke the tip off for Phoebe who was already on her hind legs, begging for a taste. The moment the bunny had the banana bit in her mouth, she happily scampered off.

"I don't know if you should feed that rabbit so much," said the housekeeper. "She's rather rotund, if you ask me."

"She's not fat," Cleo protested. She was very sensitive to remarks about the size of her pet. Besides, a tiny bite of fruit never hurt anyone.

"Not fat, my eye," mumbled the housekeeper as she stood. One thing about Nortrud, she liked to get in the last word. "So how was school today?"

"Okay," said Cleo. "There's a new kid in some of my classes, JP Edsel-Mellon."

"Edsel-Mellon?" said Nortrud with interest. "You don't mean of *the* Edsel-Mellons, do you?"

"Yeah, of *the* Edsel-Mellons," answered Cleo. "And what a snot. Said he'd read *Great Expectations* when he was nine."

Nortrud walked to the kitchen table and sat in one of the chairs. "Well, now, he probably did. I read somewhere in one of my newspapers that those Edsel-Mellon children have always had private tutors."

Cleo nibbled on her banana and nodded thoughtfully, uncertain how true this actually was. Cleo knew the "newspapers" the housekeeper was referring to were the type dismissed as "tabloid trash" by Mr. Oliver. Cleo's dad had nothing but contempt for the slick papers with sensational headlines, but no matter what anyone said, Nortrud rarely left the grocery store without buying at least one.

Cleo had to admit, the tabs were fun to read—"Bat-faced Baby Born in Oklahoma Speaks Only Russian" or "Devil Appears in Glass of Milk," *but how*, she wondered, *could anyone possibly believe all those stories were real?* She popped the last bit of the banana in her mouth and stood to throw the peel in the garbage can.

"Oh, I meant to empty that, I just didn't get a chance yet," apologized the housekeeper when she saw Cleo going to the trash can.

"No prob," said Cleo. At the Olivers, like in most New York City apartments, taking out the garbage was no big deal. The girl wrapped a twist tie around the top of the plastic bag and took it to the service entrance—the "back door" just off the kitchen.

Cleo stepped over the day's mail that was resting on the doormat in the service hallway. After dumping the trash in the large garbage can, she picked up the pile of catalogs and letters and brought it inside.

She went to set it on the kitchen counter where her parents would be sure to notice it when they got home, but first thumbed through the pile on the off chance there might be something for her. Her grandmother in Florida often sent Cleo mail for no other reason than she happened to have found a fun postcard with a rabbit on it.

But today, there was no letter from G-ma, only a bunch of catalogs, a few bills, and a couple of small notecard-sized envelopes. *Probably invitations*, thought Cleo. At the bottom of the stack of mail she found one large card that was unusually weighty and giving in to her curiosity, the girl pulled it out and looked closely at the cream-colored envelope.

The paper was a heavy rough-finished bond with plenty of gold flecks that looked and felt expensive. On top of that, the Olivers' name was written on the front in large flowery gold calligraphy. It was definitely overdone and Cleo flipped the envelope around to see who had sent such expensive stationery. A return address was embossed on the back flap of the envelope. It said simply, in gold block letters, THE EDSEL-MELLONS, NEW YORK CITY.

Chapter 3

Why would the Edsel-Mellons be sending my parents a letter? wondered Cleo. She couldn't wait to find out what this was about, especially since JP was now a classmate. When her father finally walked in the front door, Cleo pounced on him.

"Open this, Dad," she said, shoving the envelope into the man's hand. "What do you think it is?"

Scott Oliver was a lanky scarecrow of a man who worked as an independent journalist, contributing articles to *The New York Times* and other city and national publications. Cleo's father typically spent time traipsing around the city doing research and following up leads, and he usually returned home looking like he'd just run the marathon. Today was no different. His shirt was undone, his tie loosened, and his shoelaces untied—something Cleo knew wasn't done to be in style. Mr. Oliver just couldn't manage to stay neat.

He ran a hand over his permanently frazzled black hair, walked to the TV room down the hall, and plopped his six-foot-four frame onto the couch. "Can't a fellow get a proper greeting around here?" he said. "Hello would have been perfectly acceptable." He mockingly pulled down the corners of his mouth in a frown.

"Sorry, Dad," apologized Cleo. She sat on the arm of the sofa and reached over for a hug. "Hi." She slid upside down into his lap, ending up in an entanglement resembling a gigantic spider. Cleo extricated herself, then pointed to the card again. "Okay, now, Dad. Open that envelope."

Mr. Oliver ripped the card open along the side. "It's got to be an invitation," he said, adjusting the aviator-style glasses on his nose.

Cleo leaned in to read over his shoulder.

" 'The presence of you and your family is requested aboard *Natalie's Dream*' . . . blah, blah, blah. Big whoop, as you would say." He harumphed and tossed the invitation onto the end table.

"Natalie's Dream!" echoed Cleo. "I can't believe you got an invitation to go see it." The Edsel-Mellon yacht was famous for its size and extravagance, as well as the fact that only the cream of New York society was ever invited aboard. Cleo lurched over her dad to grab the card. She had never been on a really big yacht before. " 'You and your family'? That means me, too, doesn't it, Dad? We've got to go."

Cleo saw the card was signed "A fellow Walton parent," and she had a momentary flash of JP snubbing her after English class. She pushed the thought from her mind while she took another look at the card. "Oh, my gosh, the party is Thursday night."

Mr. Oliver grunted. "Talk about a last-minute invitation. It doesn't appear that we are very near the top of the guest list, does it?"

Cleo ignored the remark. The important thing was that they had been invited and if the teenager had anything to say about it, the Oliver family was going to be on *Natalie's Dream* this coming Thursday.

"Anybody around?" The musical voice made both Cleo and her dad sit up and look toward the front hall.

Mrs. Oliver rarely came home in a bad mood, no matter how hard a day she'd had at work. Alexa was a tall, willowy woman who earned her living as a model. What had first brought her to fame was her trademark chestnut hair that sparkled with hundreds of subtle shades ranging from gold to chocolate, but she was now even more well known for her cheerful personality.

"Hi, Mom. You'll never guess what came in the mail today." Cleo ran to the front hall, grabbed her mother's arm, and practically dragged her into the TV room. She waited for her parents to exchange a peck, then motioned for her mom to sit.

"You mean we got something other than junk mail for a change?" said Mrs. Oliver. She looked to her husband for an answer, but he only grunted.

"*This* is what came," said Cleo, brandishing the invitation. "Mom, we've been invited to see *Natalie's Dream*. Please, please say we can go."

Mrs. Oliver laughed and took the cream-colored card from her daughter. She opened it and read, as Cleo looked on anxiously. Finally, Alexa closed the card. "What does 'a fellow Walton parent' mean, Cleo? Are his children going to your school?"

Cleo nodded. "One, anyway." In the excitement over the invitation, she'd forgotten to mention the fact.

"Well, in that case, I definitely think we should go, don't you, Scott? We don't want to be rude to a fellow parent." She smiled at her daughter. "And it does say 'you and your family.' I suppose that means Cleo should come with us."

"Yes!" cried Cleo. She snuck a peek at her father.

"Okay, okay, okay," he said, throwing his arms in the air. "I can see I'm outnumbered here. We'll go."

"Scott, nobody's saying *you* have to go." Mrs. Oliver linked her arm around her daughter's.

"Yeah, Dad," said Cleo. "But what's the big deal, anyway?" Her father was behaving very weirdly. Anyone else would be thrilled to get an invitation like this.

Mr. Oliver cleared his throat. "Let's just say that I don't think we've suddenly made the list of the elite without a reason. I have a feeling that, as usual, someone wants something."

"What do you mean?" asked Mrs. Oliver.

"Let me give it a little more thought before I say anything else," he said. "But no matter what, I can't have you two lovely ladies going to sea all by yourselves—I see no choice but to accompany you." He smiled sheepishly. "And I hate to admit it, but I'd kind of like to get on board that baby myself."

Mrs. Oliver nodded understandingly and patted her husband on the arm. "Whatever you say, honey." She looked over at her daughter and winked. "Come on, Cleo, let's RSVP."

The girl followed her mom into the kitchen and while Alexa dialed the phone number on the card, Cleo told Nortrud about the upcoming party.

"*Natalie's Dream*. Well, well, well." The housekeeper dried her hands on a dish towel hanging from her waistband and nodded appreciatively. "That's some invitation. I'd say there would be no way to refuse that one."

"Exactly," agreed the teenager.

"Perhaps that boy will be a little friendlier if he sees you in another setting," said Nortrud. "Remember, it's hard to be a new student at a new school."

Yeah, maybe, thought Cleo doubtfully. She agreed she may have been hasty in her judgment of JP and promised Nortrud she'd try one more time to befriend the boy.

When Alexa had finished her call to the Edsel-Mellon social secretary, Cleo picked up the invitation to keep as a souvenir, then she took the phone to her room to call Robbi. She knew her friend was going to jump out of her skin when she heard about the party and Cleo was extra excited because this would be the first time her parents were allowing her to attend a big party on a school night. Maybe they were finally starting to realize that she was growing up.

Chapter 4

The next morning Cleo had far better luck getting ready for school. She put on a new white shirt and a man's vintage brocade vest that she had found in a thrift shop on the Upper East Side. Definitely an improvement over yesterday's outfit.

She noted with pleasure that today her green eyes seemed to be a cool shade of aqua and her hair, for once, was behaving. She figured today was as good as any to talk to JP and decided that right after homeroom would probably be the best time.

"Hi," she said, shifting her backpack to her left shoulder. "I don't know if I introduced myself yesterday. I'm Cleo Oliver. Remember English class? And, well, I'm coming to the party on *Natalie's Dream* Thursday night." She smiled and extended her hand to JP.

The boy ignored the offered handshake and put his hand to his glasses as if to focus them so he could stare at Cleo. "Oliver. I don't recognize the name. What does your family do? I mean, which corporation do they run?"

"Uh, corporation? I don't know what you mean. My dad's a journalist and my mom's a model." Somehow this wasn't going as she'd thought it would. "I'm sure you've heard of my mother, um, Alexa." That usually got a serious reaction, though Cleo tried to use it only as a last resort. She didn't want people liking her because her mom was famous.

There was no sign of recognition on the boy's face. "A model? And did you say your dad's a journalist? So what you're telling me is, your parents work for other people."

Cleo was taken aback, and suddenly felt very much on the defensive though she wasn't sure why. "Well, yeah, I guess you could say they work for other people, but doesn't everyone?"

"Not my father," answered JP. He lifted his nose into the air and walked off, leaving an openmouthed Cleo behind.

"Hey, what's up?" said Robbi. As usual, Cleo's friend had dashed into homeroom at the very last second. She sometimes only stuck her head in the doorway, waved to Mr. Gorgola, so she wouldn't be marked absent, then hurried straight to her first-period class.

Cleo gave Robbi a replay of the conversation she'd almost had with JP Edsel-Mellon. "It really makes me not want to go to the party at all. I mean, he was like such an absolute snob."

"Big surprise," said Robbi. "I was on to that yesterday. I don't know why you even bothered to talk to him again, but that still doesn't change a thing. No matter what, you've got to be at that party. How else am I gonna find out all the juicy details about *Natalie's Dream*?"

Cleo made a poor attempt at a laugh. "Yeah, I do sorta want to go . . . I guess."

"Think of it this way," said Robbi, "you probably won't even see JP. There'll be gobs of people there, I mean, I'll have to watch it on the weekend edition of *ET*, but you're actually going to live the eleven o'clock news. It's bound to be seriously incredible."

Robbi didn't know how right she was.

By Thursday, Cleo had talked herself back into going to the party and was even looking forward to it again. She had managed to avoid JP at school and hoped she'd be able to do so on *Natalie's Dream* as well.

After school, she'd rushed home, anxious to get her studying done before the evening's festivities. The main problem she had after that was deciding what to wear to the party. It wasn't that Cleo didn't have nice clothes. She'd been to quite a few elegant affairs with her parents, but it was that awkward time of year when the winter dresses were too wintry, and the summer dresses were, well, too summery.

But worse than that, Cleo had a horrible suspicion that everything she had would be too small. As she went into her closet she found herself wishing that she had tried on a few outfits earlier in the week.

Now that she thought about it, this was the first spring party she'd been to this year, which meant that almost for certain, nothing was going to fit. Great.

She opted for a skirt and blouse. Separates were always more forgiving to a growing girl and she slipped on a beautiful royal purple skirt that had been her favorite last year. It went on easily so she turned to check herself in the mirror. Darn. Last year, the skirt had been fashionably long, but now unfortunately it was hitting at that particular spot below her knees that made her look horribly frumpy.

Cleo examined the hem to find there was almost none to let down. The only saving factor was that it still fit around her waist. Though Cleo was growing taller, she didn't seem to be filling out that much. She reached for the lavender silk blouse that matched the skirt, but could see immediately that it wouldn't fit.

Actually, she thought, *my white shirt and vintage vest would look pretty good with the skirt*. If only she hadn't worn the two pieces already this week. How could she go to a fancy party in practically the same outfit she'd worn to school only two days ago?

Cleo took another look in her closet. There was no choice. She simply didn't have anything else that would work tonight. If she was lucky, there wouldn't be anyone from school at the ship, except, of course, JP, and Cleo planned to do her best to make sure she didn't run into him.

Cleo went to the front hall closet to pick out a coat.

After all, it would be cold outside, especially on the water. Maybe she could keep her coat wrapped tightly around herself the whole evening.

Her parents appeared a few minutes later. Mrs. Oliver was stunning, as always, in a dark coral dress that had lines reminiscent of clothes from the 1930s. She looked very retro and extremely chic.

Scott Oliver, on the other hand, was more than rumpled tonight. His twisted idea of making a protest was to wear a T-shirt and sneakers with his tux. Cleo had seen this done in some of the fashion magazines and it had worked great. But her dad hadn't managed to get it quite right. Instead of looking as if he was making a fashion statement, he looked like a fashion victim.

The three Olivers left the apartment, jumped in a cab, and rode toward Pier 46, their various long legs scrunched this way and that in the tight space of the back seat. After they finally got themselves semicomfortably arranged, Cleo turned to her father.

"Okay, Dad," she said, "what were you talking about when you said we got invited because someone wants something?"

"Well," said Mr. Oliver, glad to have an opportunity to talk, "I've thought it over and I think this party is, first of all, nothing more than a ploy to glom publicity for Edsel-Mellon's new waterfront development project." He sat up a little in his seat and cleared his throat.

Cleo couldn't help letting a small groan escape. Her father loved to pontificate and she saw the warning signs that a speech was brewing.

"Remember that article I wrote about Edsel-Mellon's housing project on the Upper East Side? After it came out the man had no choice but to give up his attempts to evict that elderly woman, Blanche Wilson, out of her home. Without her piece of property he had to walk away from his planned development.

"That's what I think this invitation is all about. Edsel-Mellon thinks if he can get on my good side, I'll endorse his waterfront project." Mr. Oliver suddenly started picking at his fingernail. "You know, I never did find out who tipped me off to that scheme."

Cleo looked down in her lap to hide the smile on her face. *She'd* actually been the one who'd left the message on her dad's voice mail telling him about Mrs. Wilson. The teenager had met the woman a few months ago and learned how Mr. Edsel-Mellon was buying up properties on the Upper East Side. He had started a false rumor that powerful electrical fields in the area were making it an unsafe place to live. As a result the developer was able to get much of the land for ten cents on the dollar.

Mr. Oliver had followed up on the "anonymous" tip, exposed the fraud in an article for *The New York Times*, and forced Edsel-Mellon to look elsewhere for a place to build his massive project. The waterfront area had become his latest target.

"You know," said Mr. Oliver as a parking attendant dressed in a gold uniform waved their taxi toward the end of the pier, "I'm very curious to see how far these people will go to get me on their side."

A majestic yacht, decorated stem to stern with colored lights, was tied up at the end of an old, partially restored wooden pier. A huge canopy that led to the gangway proclaimed NATALIE'S DREAM. No subtlety here.

"Wow," said Cleo, looking up at all the ribbons and balloons. "This is . . . awesome."

"Aw-ful would be a more appropriate word," said Mr. Oliver.

Alexa tapped her husband's arm. "Now, Scott, you promised you'd behave. We're guests after all."

Cleo had to admit, the ship was less than tastefully done, but it was also mesmerizing. It looked like Christmas, New Year's Eve, and the Fourth of July all mixed up in one spectacular holiday celebration. She followed her parents into the narrow tent that led to the yacht. The tent resembled a security checkpoint at an airport with a metal detection system, a gate for people, and a conveyor belt for packages. Several guards manned the operation, and a dark-haired woman dressed in a simple but elegant black gown stood by checking guests off a list with a slender silver pen.

Her dark red manicured nails matched her lipstick and she made quite a striking picture against the flamboyant background of *Natalie's Dream*. "Hello, I'm Elaine," she said, "the Edsel-Mellons' secretary. And you are?" The pretty lady aimed a crimson lips-only smile at the Olivers.

Cleo's dad stepped right up to the woman. "Scott Oliver and family." It came out like a challenge and

Cleo and her mom exchanged a worried look. Mr. Oliver looked like he had come eager to do battle.

"Right here," said Elaine, making an exaggerated check on her list. She gestured the family toward the ship.

"Thank you," said Cleo's mom as the family walked past.

Elaine nodded her head, then seemed to think for a moment before speaking again. "Enjoy the evening and I hope you find it in your heart to write something a bit more positive this time, Mr. Oliver."

Cleo stole a glance at her father, but he didn't acknowledge the secretary's comment so the girl decided she'd better just ignore it as well. It looked like her dad had been right about the situation—someone wanted something from him.

They walked up the gangway at a fairly steep angle over a lush red carpet, heading toward an immense flower-covered archway on the yacht's deck. Herbert and Natalie Edsel-Mellon, neither of whom were very tall, stood on a low platform, just under the center of the bower, poised as if they were the emperor and empress of New York. They were rather formally kissing cheeks and shaking hands with a clump of guests, but it became an entirely different scene when the Olivers approached. Both hosts greeted the family as if they were long-lost blood relatives. It seemed a little overdone to Cleo and she leaned away slightly in response to an overperfumed kiss from Mrs. Edsel-Mellon.

"Great of you to be here, Scott," said Mr. Edsel-Mellon. He was a portly but very distinguished-looking man with sparse gray hair and brilliant blue eyes, who looked to be in his mid-fifties. "May I call you Scott?"

Mrs. Oliver nudged her husband.

"Scott's my name," said Cleo's dad with a forced smile and a tight voice. He looked over at Mrs. Edsel-Mellon. "Nice of you to have us here."

"And I hope you'll call me Herbert," continued Mr. Edsel-Mellon. "After all, I guess you could say, we are more than just acquaintances. You know quite a bit about me, and, well, I've made it my business to find out all about you, too."

It sounded a little like a threat to Cleo, but when she looked over at the man, he was smiling broadly and genuinely. His wife was also smiling and had linked arms with Mrs. Oliver.

Cleo guessed it had been Mrs. Edsel-Mellon who had expressed herself through the decor of the boat that bore her name. The woman, a pleasingly plump, gorgeous redhead, who appeared to be much younger than her husband, was dressed appallingly in a bright pink gown with a sequined bodice and an ostrich-feathered skirt. She kept steadying a matching head-dress that looked as if it might have belonged to a Las Vegas showgirl, and to accessorize, she wore what appeared to be fifty pounds of diamonds and sapphires.

"We hope you'll think of us as good friends," Natalie Edsel-Mellon said with a slight lisp. The woman looked over at Cleo. "You must be Cleopatra. I'm sure you and JP have met at school. He's around here somewhere. Let me see if I can get him to show you around *Natalie's Dream*."

Great, thought Cleo. This was not at all what she had in mind for the evening. She wasn't that fond of the boy as it was, and he would certainly despise her even more if he was forced to take her on a guided tour of the boat. The teenager glanced around uncomfortably, glad that JP was nowhere to be seen. At that moment Mr. Edsel-Mellon made a motion with his chin, calling over a white-haired man.

"This is Hal Stuart, one of my attorneys. Hal, Scott and Alexa Oliver and their daughter, Cleopatra. Would you be so kind as to show the Oliver women the highlights of *Natalie's Dream*. Give them the hundred-dollar tour."

Thank you, sir, thought Cleo, sighing in relief.

Hal Stuart was what Cleo thought of as an old-fashioned gentleman. With his Southern accent and impeccable manners, he even looked like he should be selling chicken, but he had a reputation as one of the sharpest and most aggressive trial lawyers in the city. Cleo knew she had heard his name in connection with some of the more sensational trials in New York.

Mr. Stuart took Cleo and her mom around and told them how the 299-foot boat was only one foot short of the size of a football field, had a full ballroom, and was able to sleep fifty-five in relative comfort. The hull had been laid in Hong Kong and its magnificent interior had been completely handcrafted in South Florida from the finest hardwoods. The only drawback Cleo could see was that a chronic lapse in taste tended to overwhelm the stateliness of the grand yacht. Wherever the decor wasn't red and gold, it was purple and pink, giving the ship the look of a floating casino.

Before they knew it, the tour was over and Cleo and her mother were thanking Mr. Stuart as he returned them to the main deck. They arrived just in time to rescue Cleo's father from the clutches of a tall, reed-thin, and obviously very opinionated man.

"And who are these lovely ladies?" cooed the man as Cleo and her mom joined Mr. Oliver.

Cleo's dad made the introductions. "Pepper Charvet is the Edsel-Mellons' press agent," he explained.

"Just call me Pepper, please," said the man with a flowery gesture, utilizing his arms and hands as if he were a dancer. His hair had been sprayed and poufed to perfection and Cleo was sure he used bronzer to highlight his out-of-season tan. "I was just saying to Scott here that it seems we've both opted for the casual look." The immaculately groomed press agent pointed his foot showing off a white high-top Converse sneaker with a violin and musical notes embroidered on the side.

Cleo's face turned bright red as she, along with everyone else, looked down at Mr. Oliver's grimy sneakers. It wasn't exactly the same thing, and there was an uncomfortable silence until Alexa broke it.

"Brilliant minds think alike," she said, giving everyone an excuse to laugh and break the tension.

Pepper looked over at the skyline that was perfectly etched against the sky on the pristine, cloudless night and said, "I *do so* love this town." He turned his eyes to the Olivers, then added, "You know, I've never in my life found it necessary to go more than fifty miles from these city limits."

"Wow," said Cleo, "really? You've never gone *anywhere* outside of New York City?"

"Why should I?" said Pepper. "Everything anyone needs is here."

Boy, is that weird, thought Cleo. She loved New York herself, but she still found it fascinating to visit other places.

It looked as if the last of the guests had arrived and the boat was just about to leave the dock when a half dozen limousines turned into the pier. "Just a minute," called someone jumping out of the first car. "We're here."

Cleo watched as a group of young people stepped out of the limos and felt a growing lump of dread in her stomach. The kids were from Walton. In fact, these were the elite of the elite—the most popular members of the "in" clique at school.

"Oh, look, honey," whispered Mrs. Oliver, "those kids look like they're your age. I was just beginning to worry that you'd be the only teenager here. Are any of them from Walton?"

"Yeah, Mom," said Cleo, "they all are." She had a pretty good idea how the rest of the night was going to play out and in her mind wrote the headline for the story: "CLEO OLIVER SNUBBED ON *NATALIE'S DREAM*—ALL NIGHT LONG." At school not one of these kids had ever done so much as even glance in her direction.

She went to follow her parents, but they'd already moved off to mingle.

It wasn't long before Cleo's worst fears were confirmed. The teen clique passed through security and, in no time at all, were headed her way. Cleo tried to smile and made herself take a step forward to say hello, when she saw two of the girls start whispering and pointing in her direction.

Nervously she looked down, and was rudely reminded that she'd worn the same distinctive blouse and vest to school just days ago. Obviously, the girls had noticed.

Then she remembered the hideous length of her skirt and when she heard the girls break into peals of laughter, that was it. Not daring to look up, Cleo fled toward the darkened back area of the ship.

Chapter 5

The strings of bright lights stopped near the stern of the yacht, and though the area wasn't roped off, Cleo could see the Edsel-Mellons hadn't meant for anyone to go back there, but she didn't care. Right now what she needed was a quiet place to get herself together—and hide. There were two lifeboats that were tied down and suspended from crane arms so they could be lowered into the water. It seemed like a perfect refuge, maybe even until the party was over. Cleo sat down and closed her eyes.

A moment later, to her amazement, she heard a tiny sneeze. It didn't sound exactly like a human sneeze. More like, no, almost *exactly* like her Phoebe's sneeze though Cleo couldn't imagine that there would be a rabbit on board *Natalie's Dream*.

She wrinkled her nose and jumped back because it

suddenly occurred to her that it might have been a rat. Maybe this wasn't the place to hang out. Then she heard whispering and the voice was decidedly human.

Mustering her courage, Cleo reached out and tentatively lifted the white tarpaulin that covered the lifeboat. She peered in and, still keeping her distance, saw someone looking back at her. Inside the boat was a small girl, cowering down, clutching a tiny white puppy.

"Please don't tell," pleaded the girl who looked like a delicate porcelain doll with huge gray eyes and almost-white blond hair that curled softly around her face. She pulled the fluffy puppy in closer and gave it a kiss on the nose.

"What are you doing here?" asked Cleo.

"Nothing," said the girl. "I just don't want anyone to know I brought my dog on board." She lowered her voice to a whisper. "Pepper is allergic to dogs."

"You mean that press agent guy?" asked Cleo.

The girl nodded. "He also says they're messy and annoying."

Cleo was about to ask how the girl knew Pepper when the little dog barked.

"Shh, Bilbo," said the girl. She looked up at Cleo. "He's a little nervous. It's his first time on a boat."

Cleo smiled and reached out to pet the dog. "His name's Bilbo?" she asked.

"Uh-huh," said the little girl, "and I'm Lilliana."

"I'm Cleo. Nice to meet you." She noticed Lilliana was wearing an expensive party dress. Obviously, she was a guest here, but she evidently didn't feel comfortable if she was hiding in the lifeboats. "Um, you aren't running away or anything, are you?"

"No, of course not," said the girl. "It's just that there aren't supposed to be any pets here tonight, and Bilbo's my best friend. Now, you promise you won't tell, right?"

Thinking of her own pet rabbit, Cleo said, "You've got my word. I won't say a thing about Bilbo. What kind of name is that, by the way? I've never heard it before."

"Didn't you ever read *The Hobbit*?" asked Lilliana.

Cleo shook her head. "Actually, I think it's on one of my reading lists for later in the year." It was a little embarrassing to have to admit this to a girl who had to be years younger.

It didn't seem to make the slightest difference to Lilliana, however. "Oh, you're going to love it. You see, the hobbits are these dwarfylike creatures and they have hairy feet," explained the little girl. She held up her puppy's fuzzy paws. "Bilbo was my favoritest character in the book." She looked up at Cleo hopefully. "Do you want to sit down or anything?"

Cleo was glad for the invitation. It would be nice to spend a little time with someone who wasn't judging her on how tall she was or how badly her clothes fit. She climbed down into the boat and sat beside Lilliana.

"Gosh, you're really tall," said the little girl. "How old are you, anyway?"

So much for not noticing my height, thought Cleo. "I'm thirteen," answered Cleo. "What about you?"

"Nine," said Lilliana. "But everyone tells me I look younger and act older."

Cleo thought that the girl did sort of act older, and she seemed really smart for a nine-year-old. The two girls talked for about half an hour and in the middle of the conversation it suddenly hit Cleo why she had wanted to come to the party so desperately. It must have been a subconscious thing, but she realized now that she must have been hoping that if other Walton kids were invited, just maybe they would see how much fun she could be and what a great personality she had. Maybe they would accept her as something more than just the tall geek in the eighth grade.

But here she was, hiding out in a dark lifeboat and probably having a better time with this nine-year-old girl than she would ever have had with any of her stuck-up classmates.

"Are you hungry?" asked Lilliana. "I think the food's supposed to be pretty good tonight."

Cleo's stomach chose that moment to rumble. She felt a blush ride her face as she said, "I guess that answers your question, huh?"

Lilliana giggled. "I think Bilbo's hungry, too, but we've got to leave him here."

Cleo watched as the little girl tied the dog's leash to the lifeboat. Then she secured the canvas cover back in place.

Bilbo whimpered as the girls started to walk away, and Lilliana ran back quickly. "Oh, no. Bilbo, you've got to be quiet." She quickly untied the canvas and put a hand in to pat the dog who calmed down immediately, but as soon as she took a step away, the dog started crying again.

"I guess I'd better stay here," said Lilliana reluctantly.

"I could get some food for you and Bilbo," offered Cleo.

Lilliana smiled her gratitude as she untied her dog and wrapped her arms around him again. "Oh, that's okay. Maybe when you get back though, you could sit with him for a little while so I could go out. He seems to like you."

Cleo nodded. "No problem. I'll be back soon. I've got to find the rest room first, though, so I can wash my hands." After playing with Bilbo, she didn't think her fingers were quite sanitary.

"Oh, you mean the 'head,'" said Lilliana. "That's what they call the toilets on boats. There's one right on deck, but I'm sure it will be crowded. You should go downstairs. There's another one on the lower deck, or if that's crowded, go to the crew's quarters two flights down. That's probably the fastest. Two flights and halfway down the first hall to starboard."

Cleo was impressed with the girl's boat lingo. She wasn't quite sure what starboard was but figured she could find it. In fact, now that Lilliana had reminded her, the teenager remembered seeing the crew's quarters on Mr. Stuart's tour.

Cleo slipped back into the brightly lit section of *Natalie's Dream* and slowly mingled with the crowd, being sure to avoid the laughing group of thirteen-year-olds gathered right in the center of the deck.

The girl decided to make a quick check of the buffet tables and was pleased to see that while the requisite fancy foods like oysters, caviar, and pâté were on the table, there was also a great-looking spread of tiny hot dogs, baby burgers, and buffalo wings. Whoever had planned the buffet had known that teenagers would be among the guests.

Satisfied that there would still be plenty to eat when she came back, Cleo went down the nearest staircase she saw. A swarm of adults was coming out of the ballroom and the teen scooted to the side to let them pass, then went down the next set of stairs. When she reached the lowest deck, she was startled to overhear an angry conversation between two men with British accents.

It was a pair of ship's stewards who were clearly disgruntled over their wages. Cleo couldn't imagine that the Edsel-Mellons wouldn't pay a decent salary, but listening to the two men talk, it sounded like they were earning close to nothing.

Cleo stood unable to move as the voices got louder, then suddenly the men came bursting out of a stateroom at the end of the hall. The teenager looked around desperately for someplace to hide, but all she could do was plaster herself in one of the doorways, hoping the shadows would hide her. To her horror, when the two stewards rounded the corner, the first thing they saw was Cleo.

Chapter 6

She opened her mouth to explain, and was surprised to see that the two men who both wore spotless white uniforms were now smiling pleasantly at her. Their moods had changed as dramatically as if a switch had been thrown.

"Can I help you, miss?" asked the taller of the two stewards. "This is the crew's quarters. You must be lost."

Cleo didn't miss a tinge of suspicion in the man's tone and she instantly assumed the role of lost party guest. "Oh, yes, please. I was just looking for the rest rooms and I guess I must have taken a wrong turn." She smiled her most pathetic smile, wishing she were smaller and cuter. Robbi could get anyone to help her anytime, just because she was so petite. People somehow expected that anyone as enormous as Cleo would know how to take care of herself.

The man gestured for her to go ahead of him. “It’s straightaway up those stairs. We’ll be right behind you to make sure you get to the main deck.”

Cleo climbed the two sets of stairs with the ship’s stewards behind her all the way. When she reached the top, she turned to thank the men who both tipped their hats before going back down.

The girl’s heart was racing. Even though she hadn’t done anything but be in the wrong place at the wrong time, the encounter had given her a major adrenaline rush, something Cleo hadn’t had since the last time she’d gone out as Undercover Cleo. She took a deep breath, exhaled sharply, and set off to find the rest rooms on the main deck.

After she’d washed her hands, she returned to the buffet table and loaded up a plate with lots of tiny hot dogs and a pile of baby carrots. She turned to go back to the lifeboat area when she found herself facing Lilliana. “Hey,” said Cleo, “how did you get Bilbo to stay quiet?”

Lilliana laughed. “He fell asleep. He does that a lot, I guess, ’cause he’s still a puppy. Anyway, it gave me a chance to get to the chow table myself.” She heaped a spoonful of caviar on her plate, then served herself a healthy slice of pâté. “Mmmm. I love this stuff. You should try some.”

Cleo eyed the beige slab of steamed, pressed goose liver. She’d tried it once before and hadn’t thought much of it, but maybe this time it would be better.

Foods had a way of growing on you sometimes. She cut a judicious sliver, but decided to leave the caviar alone. She definitely did not like the salty fish eggs, no matter how much of a treat they were reputed to be.

"Will you come back to the stern with me?" asked Lilliana.

"What's that?" asked Cleo.

"The stern? The back of the ship, you know, where Bilbo is. Please? It's kind of nice having someone to talk to."

Cleo grinned. "Yeah, it is, isn't it. Come on, let's go."

Lilliana beamed as the two girls moved toward the unlit area of the deck. Neither of them noticed a person standing off to the side, watching them intently, nor did they see the person raise a small walkie-talkie and whisper into it.

What the girls did notice, moments after reaching the darkened area around the lifeboats, was the sound of several splashes coming from somewhere out on the river.

"What was that?" asked Cleo.

Lilliana shrugged. She set down her plate, then went to the edge of the railing. The tiny blond girl looked over the dark waters of the Hudson, then gasped. "Cleo, come here. Quick!"

Cleo rushed to Lilliana's side and shielded her eyes to help them adjust to the blackness beyond the edge of the railing.

"There," said Lilliana, pointing toward the pier.

A small fleet of rubber rafts was being silently

rowed from the direction of the shore straight toward *Natalie's Dream*. The boats, filled with people dressed in black, looked like a raiding party out of some James Bond movie and they were only a few yards away from intercepting the yacht.

"Cleo, I'm scared," said Lilliana. "What do we do?"

"Come on, we've got to tell someone," said Cleo. "And we'd better do it fast." She grabbed the little girl's hand and started to pull her toward the crowd on deck.

"Wait!" commanded Lilliana. "I have to get Bilbo."

"That'll take too much time," said Cleo. "We've got to tell someone now. Those people don't look like they're here to deliver flowers." Cleo yanked on Lilliana's hand and this time the girl came with her willingly.

The girls hurried into the open, brightly lit area of the main deck, Cleo frantically looking around for someone in authority. She didn't see either of the Edsel-Mellons, nor Pepper, nor the social secretary, Elaine. She couldn't even find the two stewards she had overheard. She was starting to panic when finally she saw her parents standing at the far side of the ship. Cleo knew her father would know what to do, and with Lilliana in tow, she pushed her way through the throng to get to him.

"Dad!" she called. She waved her free arm madly but Mr. Oliver was deep in conversation. Cleo kept wading through clusters of people until she finally reached her parents, but it was too late.

At that moment the band of people in black burst up over the side rail and onto the deck.

Chapter 7

Cleo screamed and dove toward her parents, pulling Lilliana with her. She raised her hand to shield her eyes, but still saw several marauders reaching into their coats.

She was half expecting to hear gunfire but the next thing she knew, she heard music and some perfectly terrible singing. Cleo took her hand away from her eyes and realized that the people hadn't pulled automatic weapons from their coats, but instead were clutching a variety of musical instruments from banjos to small keyboards. They had struck up a loud and off-key rendition of "We Shall Overcome," cleverly working the name Edsel-Mellon into the lyrics. Cleo's dad actually smiled and leaned down to tell his daughter that the hymn had been the rallying song of the civil rights movement.

The people started shouting as well. "Green Machine! Save our green! Green Machine! Save our green!"

Suddenly everyone on board the ship broke into tension-releasing laughter. The party-crashers were merely members of the Green Machine, a pacifist environmental protection group. In addition to chanting, they started passing out pamphlets and Cleo grabbed a leaflet shoved her way. From what she quickly read, the Green Machine was protesting Herbert Edsel-Mellon's plans for his waterfront development. It did kind of make sense to Cleo, though she didn't much care for the way the organization had barged onto *Natalie's Dream*—it seemed so rude. On the other hand, she had to admit, they had certainly gotten everyone's attention.

Someone squeezed Cleo's hand. It was Lilliana. In the confusion, the teenager had almost forgotten that she'd dragged the little girl along.

"Are you okay?" Cleo asked, looking down.

The girl nodded, eyes shining. "Sure. This is really exciting!"

Cleo laughed. It was exciting and it had certainly made the party more memorable. Then she noticed something strange. "Oh, no, look." She pointed to a cluster of "guests" pushing their way through the crowd. These people were pulling both guns and pairs of handcuffs from their pockets and pocketbooks.

The night was still young.

A few other guests screamed, starting a small stampede to the railings, and one man fell overboard, which only added to the shouting and confusion. Lilliana clutched Cleo's hand even tighter and watched as several guests and crew members rushed to the man's aid.

At that moment it also became apparent that the people with the weapons were security guards. They began handcuffing Green Machine members and in a matter of minutes the protesters were hurried off the yacht and onto a motor launch that sped them away toward the shore.

With the Green Machine members gone, and the man who fell into the water safely back on board, the excitement seemed to be over. Cleo watched as the sopping man was dried off, brought something hot to drink, and handed a pile of dry clothing.

"He'll be all right, won't he, Dad?" Cleo asked.

"Sure," answered her father. "That is, after they take him to the hospital for a tetanus shot or two. The Hudson is one place you don't want to go swimming. I don't even think you'll find many rats stupid enough to do that."

The party was petering out. The yacht had come about and was now headed to the docks and the cheery laughter had subdued into a low-key murmuring. It seemed everyone was counting the minutes until they could get off *Natalie's Dream.*

Cleo felt the ship bump the dock and watched the mass of party-goers surge toward the gangplank.

"Time for us to hit the road," suggested Mr. Oliver.

The girl didn't object. She knew her dad well enough to know he was anxious to get the story of the evening's events into his computer and out to the news services.

Lilliana tugged on Cleo's arm. "I'm gonna go back and get Bilbo," she said.

"Okay," said Cleo, "but I think we're just about to leave. I guess I should say good-bye, huh?"

The little girl surprised Cleo by reaching up and giving her a huge hug. "I had the best time tonight," she said. "I've never really had a friend before. Listen, do you think it would be okay if I called you sometime?"

Cleo couldn't quite understand how Lilliana could say that she'd never had friends, and she decided the girl was probably exaggerating. Cleo did it herself sometimes. It wasn't really lying, it was more like saying how things felt, as opposed to how things really were. She smiled at Lilliana. Even if the girl was only nine, it was always good to have another friend around. "Sure. I'll give you my phone number." Cleo reached into her tiny purse, withdrew a notepad and pen, then wrote down her number. "Here," she said, handing the girl the slip of paper. "Why don't you give me yours, too?"

Lilliana nodded. "Five-five-five, seventeen-thirty."

Cleo scribbled down the number quickly. "Great. I had a really nice time, too. I'm glad I met you."

Lilliana beamed and before Cleo could say another word, the little girl scampered off. The teenager turned toward her parents and saw they had already started moving toward the gangplank. She quickly fell into step beside them.

As the three Olivers walked down the ramp, they

found themselves following an elderly woman using a cane. The lady wore a dark, wide-brimmed hat and carried a canvas bag that she clutched tightly, practically covering it with her severely hunched-over body. Considering her posture and the fact that she was using a cane, the elderly lady moved with surprising speed and agility.

Something about the woman's movements struck Cleo as odd and as she leaned forward to have a closer look, she was shocked when the bag seemed to move on its own. Cleo rubbed her eyes. It was a bit late and she was definitely tired and when the teenager looked again, the woman had reached the next cab in a line of taxis.

Now how did she get to the taxis so fast? wondered Cleo. She watched as a party attendant opened the door and the woman climbed inside without a hint of any disability. As the woman reached down to sweep her skirt into the car, Cleo noticed several things: the lady had surprisingly thick, strong-looking ankles and wore scruffy black running shoes, and on her wrist was a ratty, old, large-faced watch with a worn leather strap.

The large timepiece and awful shoes seemed strange choices to wear to a fancy party, but then, thinking of her own father, Cleo shrugged. Taste was something personal after all. She followed her parents toward the next cab in line and the family was just about to step into it when they heard a child's voice.

It was Lilliana up on the deck of the yacht. "Daddy, I can't find Bilbo! Someone, please help me look for my dog!"

Chapter 8

Cleo sprang back from the taxi door and jerked her father's arm. "Come on," she cried. "Bilbo's gone."

"Bilbo Baggins?" asked her dad. "Last I heard, he was living happily in Middle Earth. Isn't that what the land of the hobbits is called?" He chuckled to himself, but this time Cleo was not amused.

"Dad, be serious for one second. Bilbo is my friend's dog. We've got to help her find him."

Mr. Oliver exchanged an exasperated look with his wife, then reluctantly motioned to the couple behind them to take the waiting taxi. "I'm sure there are lots of other people on the ship who are better equipped to search the place," he said to Cleo, but then, seeing the look on his daughter's face, he threw up his hands. "Lead the way."

Cleo hurried toward the boat, but it wasn't easy

pushing her way up the gangplank against the flow of people leaving. Before she even reached the deck, she saw the Edsel-Mellons rushing to Lilliana's side.

Wow, thought Cleo, *maybe they're not so bad after all. It's nice of them to care so much about one of their guest's pets, especially since Lilliana said there weren't supposed to be any animals on board.* What the little girl said next surprised the teenager.

"Daddy," said Lilliana to Mr. Edsel-Mellon between sniffles, "I know I wasn't supposed to bring Bilbo, but he gets so scared when he's alone and I didn't want to spend the whole party by myself either."

The Edsel-Mellons are Lilliana's parents? thought Cleo. *No wonder she knows so much about this boat and eats caviar like it's cheese dip.*

"Now don't you worry," said Mr. Edsel-Mellon. "We'll find the dog. He probably crawled down into the bilge somewhere and got stuck. That's the kind of thing animals do when they're in an unfamiliar place. Now, where did you say you left him?"

He stood up and snapped his fingers high in the air. In moments, two men, one in a security guard uniform and the other in a black suit, materialized at his side.

Lilliana pointed in the direction of the lifeboats and after a hurried conversation with Mr. Edsel-Mellon, the uniformed guard rushed off to look for the dog while the man in the suit pulled out a walkie-talkie and spoke into it as he moved to the gangplank.

He put the walkie-talkie back into his pocket, then raised his voice. "Excuse me, everyone," he said.

"Please bear with us, but we're going to have to secure the ship."

To Cleo, the man, who was of medium height and build, seemed as nondescript as humanly possible. He had hair that was neither blond nor brown but somewhere in between and a face that had absolutely no distinguishing features. He's perfect for undercover security work, thought the girl, lapsing into her people-watching mode.

For as long as she could remember, Cleo and her father had people-watched. It was a game they loved and could play anytime, anywhere. They would choose someone in a crowd and then create a story about that person's life, occupation, even personality, all based on what Cleo and her dad could deduce from their "victim's" dress, posture, manner of speech, and gestures.

Cleo watched as the undercover guard moved rapidly through the crowd, then set a chain across the walkway to the exit. "Sorry, folks," he said, "no one's allowed to leave until we've made a thorough search of the *Dream*. Might as well grab yourselves another drink and some eats. This may take a while." There were strong protests from the remaining guests as they allowed themselves to be herded back onto the deck.

In the jumble, Cleo lost sight of the Edsel-Mellons, but managed to make her way to the man in the suit. "Excuse me, sir," said Cleo, "I'm a . . . friend of Lilliana's. Where is she?"

Cleo was close to eye level with the man so he

pulled himself up a little straighter. "The family's downstairs in the stateroom, miss. They asked not to be disturbed."

"Well, I want to help her look for her dog," said Cleo.

"Miss," said the man, "we've got everything under control. It'd be best if you'd just wait over there with the rest of the folks." He pointed toward the buffet tables.

There's got to be something I can do, thought Cleo. She turned and headed toward the lifeboats. Didn't her father always say that when looking for someone or something, start at the last known location?

When she reached the area, she saw that several work lights had been put up that cast a brilliant white light across the boat and deck. Two men and two women dressed like party guests were searching with other uniformed security guards, lifting up tarps and moving boats in a methodical search for the dog. *They must be working undercover, too,* thought Cleo as she took a tentative step forward. It didn't look like anyone needed her, but maybe an extra pair of hands and eyes would come in handy.

"Hey, you," said one of the uniformed men, "we're conducting a search here. You're supposed to wait on the main deck."

"But I want to help," said Cleo.

The man stepped forward and took a closer look at the teen. "Look, it's not that we don't appreciate the offer, but you're just a kid. Better go back to your parents and let us take care of this."

Cleo bit her lip in frustration. *Just a kid? What does he know?* It was so irritating when adults acted like kids were useless. Cleo turned on her heel indignantly and went back to her parents.

"So, Sherlock," said her dad with a teasing tone, "what'd you find out?"

"Nothing, Dad," said Cleo. "They told me they don't need my help, but you know, I just feel like I should do something."

"Cleo, honey," said Mrs. Oliver, "I know you want to help, but I'd say these are professionals here. Sometimes the way to be most helpful is to stay out of the way." She patted her daughter comfortingly on the shoulder, but it really didn't make Cleo feel the least bit better.

The Olivers waited for a whole hour while uniformed and undercover security agents conducted an intensive search for Bilbo. When the guards and Mr. Edsel-Mellon finally emerged from the bowels of the ship, it was clear from the looks on their faces that the dog hadn't been found.

Suddenly a horrible thought popped into Cleo's head. "Dad, you don't think that Bilbo could have . . . fallen overboard, do you?" She knew that the puppy could easily have lost its balance on the slippery deck and no one would have heard such a small splash. Without waiting to hear her father's answer, Cleo ran to the now empty lifeboat area and peered over the railing. There was no sign of the dog, nor of anything else in the water.

Cleo didn't know whether to be relieved or not. She

knew dogs could swim, but if indeed he had fallen, how long could a little dog tread water?

"Hey, punkin," her mom said softy as she approached her daughter, "I'm sorry, but they just announced that they haven't found the dog and they're letting us all leave now. It's late, let's go." Mrs. Oliver was standing at the edge of the lifeboats. She waited until Cleo came to her side, then gave the girl a hug.

Cleo couldn't remember the last time she'd felt this bad. Poor little Bilbo. *What a terrible way to die*, she thought. *Drowning in the Hudson River. He must have been so scared.* The teenager followed her mother to the gangplank where Mr. Oliver was locked in a conversation with Mr. Abbott, an old family friend, who was the head of one of the small publishing houses in New York City. By the way her dad kept raising his voice, shaking his head, then laughing heartily, Cleo could tell she had a few minutes to run and look for Lilliana.

All the teenager wanted to do was offer the little girl some sympathy and support. Cleo couldn't imagine what it would be like to lose Phoebe. The huge rabbit was more than a pet, she was part of the family.

Cleo was just about ready to go down the stairs when Elaine, the Edsel-Mellons' secretary, came running up. The girl stepped aside and watched as the very agitated woman looked around nervously, then headed straight for Mr. Edsel-Mellon. The secretary jerked her head to the side to indicate to her employer that she needed to speak to him in private. A moment later Mr. Edsel-Mellon excused himself from the security men and went to Elaine. She turned so her back was to the people on deck, then spoke into his ear.

"What?" said Mr. Edsel-Mellon. He raised his voice. "They said what?"

The security guards circled in, and without thinking, Cleo took a step toward them as well.

"Bilbo's been dognapped?" asked Mr. Edsel-Mellon. "Is this some kind of a joke?"

No one bothered any longer to keep their voices low as they discussed the case. Cleo moved in even closer.

"Musta been those Green Machine kooks," said the man in the suit who had spoken to Cleo. He directed his gaze toward the secretary. "What'd they say when they spoke to you on the phone?"

"It was a woman," said Elaine. "Her voice was sort of muffled, but she said she had Bilbo and she wanted money. She said she'd call later with more information."

Cleo immediately thought of Lilliana. *She's got to be so nervous, but the one good thing is, Bilbo's alive.* The teen stayed a moment longer, to be sure no more information would be given, then ran down the stairs to look for her friend.

Hearing the soft lilting lisp of Mrs. Edsel-Mellon, Cleo went straight to the large stateroom, then stuck her head in the open door to see if Lilliana was there. Natalie Edsel-Mellon sat on a huge fake-fur bedspread next to the little girl. JP stood off to one side, looking fairly distressed, and on seeing him, Cleo took a step back. She really wanted to be there for her new friend, but she didn't think she could deal with the snootiness of Lilliana's brother.

While Cleo was deciding whether or not to knock on the door and enter, Mrs. Edsel-Mellon spoke again. "Don't worry," she said to Lilliana. "It's just a dog. We'll buy you another." She smiled but it was a smile that asked for more than it gave.

Lilliana looked up at her mother, then burst into tears. At this, Mrs. Edsel-Mellon put out a tentative hand and awkwardly stroked the child's angellike hair. Lilliana seemed to cringe slightly at the touch, then curled up in a ball, still sobbing.

Cleo silently backed out of the room, embarrassed at having witnessed the private moment. She felt like she'd intruded. There was something too intimate about seeing someone cry so uncontrollably.

She tiptoed up the stairs and hurried back to her parents who were just finishing up their conversation with Mr. Abbott. Cleo quietly slipped in beside her mother and managed to smile and say hello to the man.

"Well, you've certainly grown since I saw you last," said Mr. Abbott. It was the first thing everyone said to Cleo these days and the last thing she wanted to hear.

"Uh, yeah, I guess so," she said uneasily, trying to compress her spine, hoping she'd look a little shorter.

"We didn't know where you'd disappeared to," said Mrs. Oliver. "I think we'd better get you home; after all, tomorrow is a school day."

Involuntarily Cleo yawned, prompting a chuckle

from the three adults. It had been a long, stress-filled day and the thought of crawling into bed was pushing its way into the teenager's head. Cleo's dad and Mr. Abbott shook hands, then the publisher and Mrs. Oliver kissed the air beside each other's cheeks before the Oliver family went off to find their hosts.

Mrs. Edsel-Mellon had joined her husband back on deck, but Lilliana was nowhere to be found and Cleo was disappointed to have to leave the party without saying good-bye to her friend.

As the cab sped away up the West Side Highway, the teenager leaned back in the rear seat. The disappearance of Bilbo was definitely a mystery, but was it a job for Undercover Cleo?

Chapter 9

What a party, thought Cleo as she got undressed. She threw her clothes on her cuddy chair, then pulled on her favorite pajamas, a pair with pale pink stripes that alternated with rows of tiny rabbits. Cleo had long ago outgrown the pj's—the bottoms, which from the beginning had been well above her ankle bones, were now midcalf, and the sleeves ended a good four inches from her wrist. Still, the well-worn flannel was the perfect weight for these early spring nights and there was something amazingly comforting about the touch of the soft fabric against her skin.

Cleo pulled the covers back on her bed, a hand-carved, antique Chinese wedding bed she'd fallen in love with while on a trip to Singapore with her father. She had just climbed between the sheets when there was a knock on her door.

"Yeah?" she called out. "Come on in."

"Quite an evening, huh?" asked her father as he and Mrs. Oliver walked in.

Cleo nodded and sat up in anticipation. This was what she had been waiting for. The conversation during the cab ride home had been mostly about the chat with Mr. Abbott, whom the Olivers hadn't seen in a while.

"So, Dad," said Cleo, "who do you think took Bilbo?"

Mr. Oliver sat on the edge of the bed and chuckled. "Well, it's pretty hard to come up with a valid theory if you don't know any of the facts."

"Yeah, yeah," said Cleo, "I know, but if you had to come up with something, what would it be? Do you think it could have been an inside job? What about that Pepper guy? Lilliana said he hates dogs."

Mr. Oliver laughed. "He certainly seems like he would have an aversion to animals, doesn't he? Definitely not the kind of person to tolerate dog hairs or saliva on his sport coat. But the question you probably have to ask yourself is not 'who doesn't like the dog?' but 'who has something to gain by ransoming the dog?' "

"Well," said Cleo, "ransom money is something to gain."

"That's true," admitted her dad, "but it wouldn't hurt to look even deeper, say for someone who has something against Lilliana or, even more likely, against her father. Let me ask you now, who would that put on the list of suspects?"

Mrs. Oliver walked over and sat next to her husband. "Okay, I'll bite. What about someone who works for the family, but isn't happy?"

Immediately Cleo thought of the two stewards she had heard talking. They *had* seemed awfully nervous when they discovered her outside in the hallway and they had been complaining about being underpaid. Maybe they had been getting ready to grab Bilbo.

"Disgruntled employees are a possibility," said Mr. Oliver, "but they're just the tip of the iceberg. Here's another possibility: What about Mr. Edsel-Mellon himself?" He smiled smugly as if he had given himself a pat on the back.

"What?" asked Cleo. Her dad always came up with bizarre suggestions, but sometimes he was right.

"Well," said her dad, "what if Edsel-Mellon took the dog to help push through his West Side project?"

"Wait a minute," said Cleo, "there's no way you could possibly think that."

"Why not? A little girl's dog is taken and suddenly the family is perceived as a victim. The Edsel-Mellons will gain a lot of public sympathy from this."

It sounded weird but Cleo had to admit, it did make sense.

"What about those Green Machine people?" asked Cleo. They were actually the first suspects she'd thought of, but she'd wanted to let her father know she'd given it some thought before blurting out her number-one choice.

"Possibly," said her father, "but it doesn't seem in

character for an environmental group to kidnap a pet. It's too easy for a stolen animal to get sick and die."

"Yeah, but don't you think it's kind of weird that they crashed the party and then Bilbo disappeared?" asked Cleo. "Also, they're against Mr. Edsel-Mellon's project. They have a reason to dognap."

"Motive," corrected Mr. Oliver. "You've got a point, but you can't look for just the obvious."

"Nope," agreed Mrs. Oliver. "You sure can't. You also can't stay up all night." She leaned over to kiss her daughter. "See you in the morning."

Suddenly Cleo remembered the woman who had exited *Natalie's Dream* just ahead of the Olivers. Could Bilbo have been inside that wiggling bag? The teen opened her mouth to mention it, but Mrs. Oliver hushed her with a finger to her lips.

"There'll be time in the morning," said Alexa. "If I don't stop this now, you two will talk all night."

Cleo waited until her parents left, then twisted the tiny carved dragon's head on her rosewood bed. It released a narrow hidden drawer in the headboard from which she pulled a thin navy-blue book with a maroon leather binding.

It was her journal and though she didn't write in it every night, this was one of those times she wanted to remember forever. Her pen danced over the page as she put down the details of the grandiose party on *Natalie's Dream*, meeting Lilliana, and the dognapping at the end of the evening. She closed the book, then opened it for a final sentence. "But I think that my favorite part of the night was actually when Mom and Dad and I talked afterward."

Cleo spent a fair amount of time by herself during the week while most evenings her parents made their obligatory rounds of parties, show openings, and book signings. It had been great to be included in the outing tonight and then to be able to discuss it later on.

Cleo hid her journal in the secret drawer and reached for the light. She fell asleep trying to remember everything she could about the elderly woman with the bag that had seemed to have a life of its own.

The next day at Walton, Cleo grabbed Robbi the instant she entered homeroom. Though it was usually her best friend who talked a mile a minute, this time it was Cleo. She felt as though she couldn't spit the words out fast enough as she told her friend all about the ship, the party, and, most importantly, the dognapping.

"Wow," said Robbi. "It sounds like it was amazing. No wonder JP isn't here today." She stood to leave for first-period class, then plunked herself back down in her seat. "Cleo! I'll bet you can find Bilbo. Or at least"—she lowered her voice—"Undercover Cleo can."

Cleo tried unsuccessfully to hide a grin. "Yeah," she said, "I was kinda thinking about that. But the thing is, the Edsel-Mellons don't exactly need my help. They can afford to pay any ransom or hire a whole army of detectives to find Lilliana's dog." She shrugged, then stood. "Come on. We'd better get to math."

"You've got to do something," said Robbi. One thing about Cleo's friend, she loved an adventure, and she was aching to convince her friend to join the search for the missing Bilbo—no matter what the Edsel-Mellons chose to do. Just as her argument was getting into full swing, an announcement came over the PA system.

"Good morning, everyone. This is Mrs. McMillan. Would the following students please report to my office?" The headmistress for the middle school read seven names. The last one was Cleo Oliver.

"Oh-oh," said Robbi. "What do you think that's for? Have you done anything you could be suspended for? Oh, my gosh, you didn't cheat on that history test last week, did you?"

Cleo sighed. As usual, her friend was getting carried away. "Of course I didn't cheat," she scolded. "I studied like crazy for that test and you know it." Cleo had been very proud of the B+ she'd received on the exam since history wasn't exactly her best subject.

"Well, you must have done something," declared Robbi. Her stare bored into Cleo's eyes as if that would pressure her friend into revealing any misdeed she might have committed.

"Thanks a lot, Rob," Cleo said sarcastically. She couldn't think of anything she'd done wrong, but it didn't matter—her heart was still racing.

Robbi reached out and gave her friend a squeeze on the arm. "I'm sure everything will be okay. At least, I think so." She gave Cleo a thumbs-up sign, then turned and raced down the hall to math class.

Evelyn McMillan was the headmistress for Walton's middle school. The gray-haired lady looked like the epitome of a stern schoolmarm, but in actuality she was very understanding and quite accessible to the students. Still, it wasn't comforting to be called away from classes into the woman's office first thing in the morning.

Cleo trudged down to the first floor, then slowly entered the open door to the office. Ms. Appleby, Mrs. McMillan's secretary, sat behind her desk. There were six other students gathered in the small outer office, sitting or leaning against the walls. Cleo realized they were all students who had attended the Edsel-Mellon party the night before. The same two girls who had so rudely whispered about her were there and they went into the same routine once again before breaking into giggles.

I really need this, thought Cleo. At the same time she could tell from the restless and uptight body language that every single student in the room was nervous.

The secretary nodded to Cleo, then pushed the intercom button on her desk. "They're all gathered now, Mrs. McMillan. Shall I send them in?"

The voice came over the small box. "Yes, Alice. Thank you."

"Through the door, everyone," said Ms. Appleby.

The kids looked anxiously at each other, then en masse went into the headmistress's inner office. Seated in front of the woman's desk was one of the largest men Cleo had ever seen. He stood up, overturning his chair in the process, then swiveled to face the students.

"Good morning, kids," he said in a sweet, high-pitched voice that was at total odds with his enormous stature. "I'm Detective Todd Milton."

Cleo did her best to keep her jaw from falling open.

A few months before she'd had a number of encounters with the policeman when he had been assigned to a case involving thefts at a theater on Broadway. Posing as an informant named "Nicki," Undercover Cleo had helped Todd Milton find the thief, and as a result, the man had been promoted to full detective.

"Students," said Mrs. McMillan, "we understand each of you was on board *Natalie's Dream* last night and you may be aware that the Edsel-Mellons' dog was stolen during the party. Detective Milton needs to speak with each of you regarding the disappearance of the animal."

"Don't worry, kids," said the man with a chuckle as he picked up the chair, "nobody here's in any trouble. I just want to ask you a few questions, but I'd prefer to do it one at a time." He gestured to one of the girls who had laughed at Cleo. "Miss, if you would please stay? The rest of you, if you don't mind, would you please wait in the next room?"

As they stepped back into Ms. Appleby's office, the other kids clustered together, whispering nervously among themselves. Everyone was wondering what kind of questions the man would ask, everyone except Cleo. Now that she knew why she had been called to the headmistress's office, the teen had a whole new problem to worry about.

Last fall, she had actually sat down face-to-face with Detective Milton. She had been in disguise as "Nicki," a street urchin informant, but Cleo was always worried that someone would see through her costumes. Even though Todd Milton was a bit of a bumbler, he *was* a detective, who spent hours and hours trying to connect all the dots that lead to solving a mystery, and he might just be able to identify the streetwise "Nicki" as schoolgirl Cleo.

The teen ended up being called in last and as she stepped into the room, she could feel a band of sweat break out on her forehead.

"Well, since I've spoken to all the other kids, you must be Cleo Oliver," said the policeman.

Cleo smiled weakly. "Yeah."

As the detective smiled and began his inquiry, the girl realized that her fears had been completely unfounded. Todd Milton was all business and Cleo simply answered the routine questions about what she had seen on the boat, and who she had spent the evening with.

"Okay," he said finally, "that's it. Sorry for pulling you out of class, but I appreciate your cooperation."

Cleo stood to go, then turned back. "Um, Detective Milton?" she said.

"Yes?"

The teenager had been debating whether or not to say anything about the elderly woman because she really wasn't sure whether the lady's handbag had moved or not. On the other hand, it just might be something. Before she could talk herself out of it, Cleo reeled off all the details she could remember about the woman with the cane and the kicking bag.

"Thanks," said the detective when Cleo was finished. "That's very interesting. It just might prove useful."

Cleo let herself relax and felt the tension drop out of her shoulders. "Can I go now?"

"Sure, but would you mind giving me a phone

number where I can reach you, just in case I have any more questions."

After giving the officer the information, Cleo was excused and headed straight to math where, in a series of passed notes, she assured Robbi that all was fine. With four of the other six students who had attended the party also in math class, the air was positively snowy with tiny scraps of paper flying through the room whenever the teacher turned her back. By the time class was over, it seemed everyone was talking about the dognapping incident.

In fact, it became the school's number-one topic of conversation for the rest of the day. Cleo found herself running over the events of the previous evening, but try as she might, she couldn't come up with a motive or a likely suspect and she even found herself wondering if she had done the right thing when she pointed Detective Milton's sights toward the elderly woman. Other than a possibly wiggling bag, there was no evidence and she couldn't think of any reason to link the elderly woman to the crime. What if she was totally innocent?

Cleo walked home feeling horribly guilty and worrying that the police would start harassing the old woman. Just as she entered her apartment, she heard the phone ring and then stop as someone picked it up. A moment later Nortrud called out.

"Cleo? Is that you?"

"Yes, Nortrud," answered Cleo.

"It's for you," the woman said as she bustled out of the kitchen. "Says her name is something or other Edsel-Mellon."

Chapter 10

"Be right there," said Cleo, hurrying to her room to drop off her backpack. A moment later she was in the kitchen picking up the phone. "Hello?"

"Hi," said a very young voice. "It's me, Lilliana. Do you mind that I called? I just need someone to talk to."

Cleo was surprised at how glad she was to hear from the little girl. "No, it's fine," she said. "Any news on Bilbo?"

"No. The police are trying to find him. They were here this morning asking for the guest list. They said they had one good tip about an old lady who walked all bent over and used a cane. Natalie said that the reason they think it's a good tip is that no one who looked like that was invited."

The question popped out before Cleo could stop herself. "You call your mom Natalie?"

"She's not my mom," said Lilliana. "She's my stepmom."

"Oh," said Cleo. She had other friends whose parents were divorced and despite all the fairy tales of evil stepmothers, she had yet to actually come across one. "Well, she seems nice. She's also really . . . colorful."

"Definitely," said the little girl with a laugh. "Daddy let her do whatever she wanted to the boat, but I'm glad he hired somebody else to decorate our house." Her voice got a little softer. "Maybe sometime, you might want to come over."

The girl's tone made Cleo realize how lonely Lilliana was, and how much she needed a friend. "Yeah, I'd like that," she said, then decided not to wait for "sometime" to get together. "Listen, Lilliana, would you like to meet me for some pizza?"

"Wow," said the girl. "That'd be great. You mean, like today?"

"Uh-huh," said Cleo. "If it's okay."

There was a slight hesitation before Lilliana answered. "No problem. Where should we meet?"

"Well, where do you live?"

The girl said she lived on the East Side. Cleo thought quickly. She was older than Lilliana so it would probably be easier, as well as safer, for her to travel to meet the little girl. "Well, how about somewhere around you. Do you have any pizza places you like?"

"Um, not really," said the girl. "I mean, I don't know. We don't get to eat at that kind of place much."

Cleo couldn't believe it. *How could anyone live without having pizza at least once a week?* "Is there someplace else you want to meet?"

"No," said Lilliana. "Pizza sounds like fun. Let's go to a place you know. I can have Carl take me anywhere."

Since Lilliana had transportation, Cleo gave the girl directions to The Pizza Palace, the number-one hangout for Walton students. "It's a cool place," she assured the little girl. "What do you say we meet in half an hour?"

Thirty minutes later Cleo was at The Pizza Palace, squishing herself into the crowded entry where customers waiting for take-out mingled with people waiting to pay their bills. Yet another group of Upper West Siders were biding their time until they could be seated in the always-packed restaurant.

"Hey, Cleo! How ya doin'?" The booming voice came from a large man with a dark bushy mustache.

"Hi, Bart," said Cleo, waving to the man.

Big Bart was the owner/chef of The Pizza Palace and he knew every one of his regular customers by sight. He wiped a chunky hand across his apron, then raised it in a salute before disappearing into the kitchen.

One of the servers pointed out a table in the back and just as Cleo started toward it, Lilliana walked in. "Cleo!" she called. "I made it." She ran to the teenager and gave her a big hug. "I couldn't find Carl so I had to sneak out of the house and get in a taxi. I never had so much fun in my life!"

Cleo had a moment of panic. "Lilliana, you snuck out? What are they going to do when they find out you're gone?" The teenager had a vision of an army of NYPD officers searching for a kidnapped Edsel-Mellon child and what would happen when they found her sitting in The Pizza Palace opposite Cleo Oliver! *I'd better not get arrested for this,* she thought.

"As long as I'm home for dinner, no one will ever know," said Lilliana. "They'll think I'm in my room. It's just that, well, JP and I are supposed to go everywhere with a chauffeur, that way the driver can keep an eye on us. Natalie picked out one car with a driver just for us."

Cleo remembered seeing the gold car and Carl, the pistol-packing chauffeur. "Yeah, we saw JP arrive at school in that limo." She tilted her head and looked at Lilliana. "Hey, how come you don't go to Walton?"

"Oh, well, I still have tutors at home."

It suddenly made sense to Cleo why Lilliana was so starved for friendship.

The little girl continued, "Daddy doesn't want me to go to school until I'm eleven, like JP."

It was impossible for Cleo to disguise her shock. "Your brother is only eleven? How come he's in eighth grade?"

Lilliana shrugged. "I don't know. Good tutors, I guess."

At that point, the server arrived to take their order. The girls each asked for a plain slice and a soda, then

Cleo decided it was time to change the subject. "Have you heard from the kidnappers again?"

"No," said the girl, "but they're supposed to call tonight. Daddy was going to take us to see our new country house this weekend, but Natalie said we should stay here because of Bilbo." Her eyes welled up. "Cleo, you don't think they'll hurt him, do you?"

Cleo reached across the table to pat the girl's arm. "I'm sure he'll be okay." After a moment the teen detective decided to probe a little. "What about those people from the Green Machine?" she asked. "Did anyone find out if one of them took Bilbo?"

"It's the first thing the police thought of," said Lilliana, "but they arrested all the protesters on the boat and nobody took a dog to jail."

Cleo took a bite of pizza and chewed while she pondered who else might have taken the dog. "Lilliana," she said, "you said you snuck Bilbo on board with you, right?"

The girl nodded her head.

It had occurred to Cleo that if this was a planned dognapping, the culprits had to have known the dog would be on board. "Is there anyone who knew you were going to take Bilbo to the party? Or maybe someone saw you sneaking him in," she suggested.

"No," said Lilliana. "At least, I don't think anyone saw me this time."

"What do you mean, 'this time'?" asked Cleo.

"Well, Natalie saw me once, but she was really nice about it. She said it would be our secret, 'cause she had a dog when she was little and she understood."

Cleo didn't know if this was a strike for or against Natalie Edsel-Mellon. The woman didn't seem at all malicious and she certainly didn't need any ransom money, but then again, maybe this wasn't about money.

"How long has Natalie been your stepmom?" asked the teen detective.

"Oh, about a year, I guess," said Lilliana. She looked up from the pizza that she'd been pulling apart more than eating. "Can I ask a question?"

"Sure," said Cleo.

"What's it like having a real mom? I mean, my mother died when I was two. We've always had nannies and now there's Natalie, but, well, you saw, she's not really like the moms you see in the movies."

Cleo thought of her own mother and of Robbi's mom. Neither of them was exactly like a movie mom either. Mrs. Richards was home for meals with the family, but as an actor, she tended to keep strange hours. She was also queen of the ditzes and regularly lost her keys and only made it to half her appointments on time. Cleo knew that Robbi didn't depend on her mother for much and, in fact, often seemed to have taken over the parental role herself.

Then there was Alexa Oliver. Unlike movie moms, she didn't cook, she didn't clean, she wasn't even home all that much. On the other hand, Cleo knew her mom tried to be understanding of her daughter's problems and did her very best to be a good mother. Mrs. Oliver would drop an appointment with the President of the United States if Cleo needed her for anything, and maybe that was more important than actually being home every night.

Cleo sighed. Maybe there actually wasn't such a thing as a conventional mother. She looked at Lilliana who was waiting patiently for an answer. "What's it like having a real mom? It's kind of hard to describe. Sometimes good, sometimes bad. Mostly good, I guess." She shrugged.

"That's what I thought," said Lilliana seriously.

Cleo reached across the table to give the girl's hand a squeeze. It must be horrible to have a pet stolen, then not even have a mother to go to for a hug. "Well, if you ever want to borrow my mother, you can," she said.

Lilliana laughed. "That's okay. Natalie's doing pretty good, I guess. She's the only one who misses Bilbo like I do. I think some of the other adults are glad he's gone."

Cleo perked up at this information. "Like who?" she asked.

"Oh, like Pepper mostly," said Lilliana, "but the housekeepers didn't like poor Bilbo either. Said he was chewing things and tearing up the house too much." She thought for a moment. "And the butler said he was always afraid he'd step on Bilbo."

"Didn't *anybody* like him?" asked Cleo. She couldn't imagine anyone not falling in love with the tiny puppy right away.

"Oh, they liked him, he was just a lot of trouble. He ate one of Elaine's purses one day. I don't think she was too happy about that."

It didn't sound like many in the Edsel-Mellon household were disappointed at the loss of the puppy, which probably made it even harder for the little girl. Maybe there *was* something Cleo could do to help.

When the girls finished their pizza, the older girl flagged down a cab for Lilliana. "Now you're sure you'll be okay?" she asked before she closed the door.

"Yes," said Lilliana. "Thanks, Cleo."

"Sure." Cleo shut the door, then waved good-bye as the cab sped off down Broadway.

By the time she got home, Cleo decided that she wanted to get involved in this case, if only to satisfy her own curiosity. Who had taken Bilbo? Was it Pepper with his passionate dislike of dogs? Was it Natalie? What if the woman hoped to win favor with Lilliana by getting her pet back?

Then again, it could be another one of the other Edsel-Mellon employees or, as her father had suggested, even a business enemy, of which there had to be hundreds of candidates to choose from.

Cleo took the phone to her room to make a few calls, then with a huge smile on her face, she riffled through her closet. Time to create a new disguise for Undercover Cleo.

Chapter 11

Saturday morning Cleo rose early. It had been a good while since she'd gone on an undercover "operation" and she was unusually nervous. She washed her face and went to the kitchen where her mother was poking around in the refrigerator.

"Morning, sweetie," said Mrs. Oliver as she pulled a grapefruit and some bread out of the fridge. "Can I get you something?"

"No, thanks, Mom," said Cleo. Nortrud didn't come in on the weekends, and on Sunday it was Mr. Oliver's self-appointed task to make the morning meal. That left Saturday as the one time Cleo could have anything she wanted, from a bowl of cereal to leftover pizza.

This morning she opted for Pop-Tarts and a carton

of yogurt. She took her breakfast to the table where Mr. Oliver sat reading the Saturday *Times*.

"What do you have planned for today?" he asked.

Cleo almost choked before she realized he was merely asking a simple question. "Um, nothing much. Maybe go out with Rob," she answered. "What about you?" It never hurt to know where her parents were going to be, especially if she had to sneak in or out of the house.

"Oh, I thought I'd spend a little time straightening up my office," said her dad.

Cleo dropped her jaw and clapped the palms of her hands to her cheeks. "You're going to what?" she asked jokingly.

Scott Oliver's office was the bane of both Nortrud's and Mrs. Oliver's existence. Cleo's dad made absolutely no attempt to maintain any sense of order in the cluttered space. He had stacks of papers, books, and magazines everywhere and was forever ripping articles out of the newspapers to add to the mess. "Nesting material" was what Mrs. Oliver called the piles of papers and pamphlets her husband carried into the room and rarely, if ever, took out.

"I think I want to get a videotape to record this moment," said Mrs. Oliver.

Cleo's father curled his lower lip out in mock hurt, but even he had to laugh. "Okay," he said, "I was going to invite you both to the movies this afternoon, but seeing how mean you're being to me . . ."

The Olivers were planning to see a romantic comedy with one of Cleo's favorite stars and the girl was tempted to drop her afternoon plans. After all, no one really needed Undercover Cleo to go poking about especially since the police were already on the case.

Just then, Phoebe nudged Cleo's ankle hard, hoping for a handout. The girl leaned over with a nibble of Pop-Tart, then stroked the rabbit's floppy ears and thought about Lilliana missing her poor Bilbo.

Reluctantly Cleo told her dad she'd have to pass on the movie. Even if she learned nothing today about the dognapping, at least she would have tried to help.

The night before she'd pulled several items of clothing from her mother's and father's closets, and once her parents left she rapidly dressed in her own button-down shirt and jeans. Then she put on one of her father's ties and her mother's tweed blazer.

From her closet, she took a heavy cherrywood box with brass corners and hefted it onto her dresser. The box had been a gift from a makeup artist Cleo had met in Paris at the beginning of the school year and it was filled with all sorts of makeup. Jean-Luc had taught the teenager a wealth of makeup lore while she was assisting him during one of her mother's fashion shows.

Cleo quickly applied a foundation slightly darker than her own pale skin, then added a few freckles. After shading bluish sleep-deprived circles under her eyes, Cleo added a touch of eye makeup and natural brownish lipstick to her face. She squinted, then expertly drew in a few age wrinkles, just enough to add ten years or so to her face. Next, she slicked back her hair and donned her great-grandfather Oliver's fedora.

Now Cleo put on a pair of antique wire-rimmed glasses she'd found among the rubble in her father's office, then looked in the mirror to appraise her work. Staring back was a familiar face, but not really her own. It was "Josie Silverman," eager young reporter.

Cleo had used this disguise once before and found "Josie" remarkably useful. She hoped the character would be as successful today.

The girl checked her mother's old leather bag to be sure she had her supply of journalist's "tools"—clipboard, legal pad, pencils, microcassette recorder, and, most importantly, one of her father's old press passes that she'd carefully doctored with "Josie's" picture and name. Satisfied that she had everything, she slung the bag over her shoulder and left the apartment.

Cleo rushed to the subway station at 72nd Street and rode the number 1 train all the way down to SoHo, an area of Manhattan named because it was "south of Houston Street." Full of art galleries, coffeehouses, and trendy fashion boutiques, SoHo was also home to the offices of the Green Machine.

"Josie" walked to Wooster Street and found the address she was looking for—a small innocuous building wedged in between two warehouses. She went up to the third-floor headquarters and knocked on the door.

A moment later a young man appeared in the doorway. "Yes?"

Cleo could hear new age music playing in the background. "Hello. I'm Josie Silverman, a reporter with *The New York Daily Press*." She quickly flashed her press pass so the man couldn't get a close look. "I called yesterday about interviewing Mr. Carson?"

The man nodded. "Oh, yeah, Don told me you'd called. Come on in." He opened the door wider and let Cleo pass through.

The room was brightly lit, but the Green Machine had obviously not wasted any money on decor. The white walls had peeling paint, and the bare hardwood floors looked like they could use a good cleaning as well as waxing. The room was full of cheap metal desks, folding chairs, and filing cabinets, and everywhere were stacks of papers. Cleo thought of her dad—he'd be right at home in this workplace.

"Ms. Silverman." A rosy-cheeked, jovial-looking man walked out, hand extended toward Undercover Cleo. "I'm Don Carson and as you probably know, I'm president of the Green Machine." The man looked to be in his mid-forties and was dressed in jeans and a plaid shirt.

"Thank you for seeing me, Mr. Carson," said "Josie." "Is there someplace we can talk?"

"Absolutely." The man led her to a desk in the back. "It's a good day for you to stop by. We're not so busy on Saturdays. Most of our people are out planting, especially during this time of the year."

Cleo looked around and saw that in addition to the young man who had opened the door, there was only one other person in the room, a young woman who was answering phones and working on a computer. "Out planting?"

"I don't know how much you know about our organization, Ms. Silverman, but we're very concerned with the greenery in this city. Saturdays, we ask our members and their families to tend the trees and planted plots we maintain, as well as do volunteer work in the parks throughout the five boroughs. To us these are what we call 'victory gardens.' Not so much to provide vegetables like the victory gardens of World War II, but to provide beauty, the scent of growing things, oxygen for the air, and an ambience of nature in this world of concrete. We like to say that every plant growing in this city is a little victory for the people who live here."

Impressed, Undercover Cleo took a legal pad and pencil from the briefcase she'd borrowed from her father. "I have to admit, Mr. Carson, I don't know a lot about the Green Machine. It does sound like a very worthy organization." She shifted her position and poised her pencil to write. "Unfortunately, I'm not here to do an article about the group. What I am here for is to investigate the dognapping that occurred Thursday night aboard *Natalie's Dream*."

Don Carson shook his head. "A shame. What a horrible thing, to steal a child's pet."

"So, you're saying your organization does not support taking that sort of action, a kidnapping or dognapping, to make a point?"

"Ms. Silverman," said the man, "I think I see what you're insinuating, but I must tell you that the Green Machine is a nonviolent group. Among other things, we happen to be firm supporters of animal rights."

"But you did stage a protest the night of the party, did you not?" asked Cleo.

"Of course, we protested," said Mr. Carson. "The construction proposed by Herbert Edsel-Mellon is a crime being perpetrated against the people of this city. He intends to plow under seven of our garden plots and in their place put up a row of glass, steel, and concrete skyscrapers. The plans for the entire twenty-five acres includes only one park half the size of this room." He stopped smiling and looked into Undercover Cleo's eyes. "Yes, we crashed a party, we raised our voices in a song of protest, but did you see anyone hurt or even threatened? As I said, Green Machine is committed to a policy of nonviolence."

Mr. Carson's heart seemed to be in his words, and "Josie" believed him. Unfortunately, the fact that the protest happened just prior to the disappearance of Bilbo seemed too much of a coincidence for Undercover Cleo to just let it drop.

"How did you choose that particular night for your protest?" she asked.

"Let me think," said the man. "It was a bit of serendipity, as I remember. We'd actually planned to do the protest at Edsel-Mellon's midtown offices, but about a month ago a new member joined us and she'd found out that there was going to be this big bash on Edsel-Mellon's yacht. Jeannette something or other, I can't remember her last name. She came up with this great idea for us to stage our protest on *Natalie's Dream*. She thought it might get our cause noticed." He smiled. "Boy, was she ever right. We've received a wheelbarrow full of letters of support and donations every day since the story hit the papers."

"Josie" tried to contain her excitement. So a new member had suggested the protest aboard the yacht. A coincidence? Undercover Cleo doubted it. Maybe there was a connection to the dognapping. She took a second to push up the glasses that were slipping down her nose.

"Would it be possible for me to speak with this Jeannette?" she asked.

"Well," said Mr. Carson, "she's not in today. As I said, Saturday most of our members are out 'in the field' so to speak, but Denise over there might know when Jeannette will be in."

The man walked "Josie" over to the young woman at the computer. "Denise, this is Josie Silverman. She's a reporter who'd like to speak with Jeannette." Mr. Carson shook the "reporter's" hand, then left the two women alone.

Denise tapped the keys of her computer. "Jeannette's supposed to be covering the phones this Tuesday afternoon," she said, "but I wouldn't count on it."

"What do you mean?" asked Undercover Cleo.

"Well, I'm a little worried about her. Jeannette was supposed to come in yesterday but she never showed. In fact, no one's seen her since Thursday night. I thought she rowed out with everyone on the protest, but she didn't get arrested. I don't know what happened. Maybe she got cold feet before we got into the boats, who knows. The only thing I can think of is that she feels guilty that we all went to jail and she didn't and she's afraid to show her face around here."

Undercover Cleo suddenly had an idea. "Would this Jeannette be an older woman who walks with a cane?"

"A cane?" said Denise with a laugh. "Hardly. Jeannette is about forty-five, maybe fifty, but she's one of the strongest women I've ever seen. I doubt she'll ever need a cane."

"Josie" was disappointed, but tried not to let it show. "Look, do you happen to have her phone number or address?"

Denise pushed a button and the printer spat out a sheet. "Here," she said, "this is her reach number."

"Thanks," said "Josie." "You've been a big help."

After saying her thank-yous and good-byes, Cleo headed back uptown. She caught an express train and when she glanced at her watch, she realized the entire trip had taken less than two hours. She'd probably beat her parents back from the movies.

As the train roared from stop to stop, Undercover Cleo wiped the makeup from her face, took off the tie and blazer, then put on her own sweatshirt jacket. By the time she got back to the lobby of her apartment building, "Josie" had transformed back into Cleo Oliver.

She couldn't wait to get to the phone and headed straight to the kitchen. Cleo dialed the number for Jeannette Collins and held her breath. To her great disappointment, she heard three musical notes signifying that the call hadn't gone through, then a recording came on saying that there was no forwarding number and no further information was available.

Back to square one, thought Cleo. *Jeannette Collins might not even be the woman's real name.* She'd never find her. She returned her parents' clothes, then went back to her room and repacked her makeup case. What had ever possessed her to think there was the slightest thing Undercover Cleo could do with this mess?

Chapter 12

Cleo had plans with Robbi for Sunday. The two girls were going shopping with another friend of theirs, Alyssa Goldstein. Cleo had known Alyssa forever, or at least it seemed that way. The Olivers and Goldsteins were old family friends and the two girls had practically grown up together. They'd been best friends for years, and when Robbi had transferred to Walton they had become an inseparable threesome—at least for a while.

Almost overnight, something happened this year to change the status quo—Alyssa had become beautiful. The auburn-haired girl was suddenly one of the most popular kids at school, sought after, invited to every party, and asked to join every after-school organization. Cleo couldn't really blame her old friend, but it did hurt that Alyssa sometimes didn't take the time to talk to her at school.

Still, on occasion, the girls got together for weekend activities. Today, they were headed to Macy's. There was usually something special going on at the giant department store that took up a whole huge city block and now was the time of the annual Flower Show.

For two weeks every spring, the street-level floor of Macy's was jam-packed with flowers in bloom from all over the world. Though Cleo didn't consider herself a big outdoors person, she loved flowers, and for the special event the department store put together a forest of imported orchids, roses, tulips, bougainvillea, and more. After the bleakness of winter in the city, a visit to this tropical paradise of exotic plants and wonderful fragrances was heaven, and made Cleo feel like spring and summer were just around the corner.

As the girls wandered the cosmetics counters, they let roving models spritz them with perfume samples and before long Cleo, Robbi, and Alyssa were smelling like flowers themselves. Then, at Robbi's insistence, they rode down to the Cellar where they sampled all sorts of food from cheeses to chocolates. Finally, when they were sure they'd seen everything there was to see on the main floor, and tasted everything there was to taste in the basement, the girls rode the escalators upstairs to savor the real attraction of the famous store—clothes, clothes, and more clothes.

Alyssa tried on fifteen separate outfits before settling on a beautiful summery dress. "What do you think?" she asked, modeling for her friends.

Cleo and Robbi both nodded their approval and Cleo felt a tinge of jealousy that her friend looked so pretty in the fluttery style. She knew the particular cut of the bodice would only make her look even taller and gawkier. Alyssa was one of the lucky ones. She could wear almost any of the latest fashions and look great. What was more, she seemed to be able to afford them.

Cleo looked longingly in the mirror at the pale peach blouse she held up in front of her. She was sure the sleeves were long enough. As she stood there trying to decide whether or not to spend her money on something that she would certainly outgrow within a few months, Robbi announced that she wanted to go look at shoes. Cleo's best friend had a wardrobe full of off-beat pieces from the seventies or eighties, mostly stuff she had found in thrift stores, but occasionally Robbi did splurge on what Cleo thought were weird-looking shoes. Alyssa, just-purchased dress in hand, was also eager to look for a matching pair of shoes.

"You two go on ahead, I'll meet you in a few minutes," said Cleo. The blouse was so tempting, and she really wanted to try it on. As Robbi and Alyssa went off toward the shoe department, Cleo headed to the changing rooms. On her way she noticed a woman holding a little girl's hand.

"But when can we go, Mom?" the girl asked.

"What did I say?" replied the mother. "We're going

home right after we find a dress and then you can see Fluffy again. You can't drag a kitten all over New York City. She'll be just fine staying by herself for a while."

"But she misses me," said the girl and her expression was so much like Lilliana's that Cleo felt a pang of guilt.

Maybe she'd given up too soon on Undercover Cleo's attempts to find her friend's dog. With a deep sigh and a last look at the peach blouse, Cleo hung it back on the rack and then hurried off. There were more important things to spend her money on.

She went to find her friends in the shoe department, and saw Robbi had three pairs in front of her and Alyssa had six. Cleo knew she had oodles of time to run a quick errand.

She told her friends she'd meet them in half an hour on the main floor, then hurried down the escalator. She ran across 34th Street, dodging cars, buses, and taxis, and went into Woolworth's. It was the perfect place to get what she needed for a series of Undercover Cleo expeditions.

The teen detective raided the makeup aisle, filling her shopping basket with false eyelashes, fake nails, and a few unusual colors of eye shadow and lipstick. She didn't have the slightest idea what turns this adventure might take so just in case she picked out two shades of foundation she knew she didn't have. When she got to the checkout counter, Cleo was surprised to find that all her purchases had totaled less than half what she'd contemplated spending on the blouse. It was definitely a bargain, but she sighed as she counted out the money. She had really wanted the beautiful shirt.

She hurried back to Macy's where her friends had just finished up in the shoe department. Alyssa now carried another shopping bag that she was anxious to show to her childhood friend. "But, Cleo," said the girl, eyeing her friend's bag, "why did you go into Woolworth's?" Alyssa wrinkled her nose.

"I *love* Woolworth's," exclaimed Robbi. She did, too, but Cleo knew the remark was meant mostly to tell Alyssa that not everyone believed Macy's and Bloomingdale's were the only stores in New York.

Alyssa took the hint. "Well, what did you buy?"

Cleo knew her purchases looked strange, but there was no getting out of showing her two friends what she'd bought. Reluctantly, she undid the staple at the top of her plastic shopping bag and opened it for the other girls' inspection.

Robbi knew immediately what the makeup meant: her friend was going to resume her undercover activities to solve the dognapping. "That's great," she said with a building excitement. "So I guess you're definitely . . ."

Cleo threw Robbi a hard glare. There was no point in making Alyssa aware of Undercover Cleo's projects. "Yeah," said Cleo, "I am definitely going to . . . take a makeup course." She looked at Alyssa and smiled. "There's this class that one of Robbi's mom's friends is teaching on . . . stage makeup."

Alyssa nodded her head. "Oh, yeah, I think I've heard of that class."

Cleo knew the girl couldn't really have heard of the class because she had just made the whole thing up.

"But really, Cleo," continued Alyssa, "should you be using that cheap makeup?"

"Well, you know, a lot of this is just what my mom uses. A big price tag doesn't always mean it's any better." As Cleo hoped, this shut Alyssa up since the girl thought anything Alexa did was the ultimate.

The girls walked to the street where Cleo and Robbi waved good-bye to Alyssa, who hailed a cab to take her home to her family's Upper East Side apartment. Then the two friends descended the stairs to the 34th Street subway station and caught the train uptown. They were strolling toward Cleo's apartment when they noticed the gold Rolls-Royce parked across from Cleo's building.

"Isn't that JP's car?" asked Robbi.

"It's got to be," said Cleo, "but what do you think it's doing here?"

The girls approached slowly and were somewhat alarmed when the car made a sudden U-turn and pealed to a stop beside them.

"Get ready to make a run for it," said Robbi under her breath.

Just then, the back window lowered. Cleo expected to see JP, but it was Lilliana who stuck her head out. "Cleo!" called the girl. "It's me. Um, I just wanted to talk for a little while, if you don't mind."

"Uh, well . . ." Cleo looked at Robbi, who seemed

disappointed that their afternoon together would be interrupted. "Listen, do you mind if Robbi comes along? She's my best friend."

Lilliana shook her head. "Sure, it's okay. Do you want to walk in the park?"

Cleo remembered what the girl had said about not going anywhere without a chauffeur and she wondered how Lilliana would be able to take a walk through such a public area like Central Park, but she nodded. "Sure."

It seemed like Carl the chauffeur appeared by magic. He had quietly slipped out of the car and come around to open the back door for Lilliana, taking Cleo and Robbi by surprise. The little girl hopped out and together the three girls crossed Central Park West and walked along the park.

"Don't tell anyone," said Lilliana, "but last night Daddy got a ransom note for Bilbo."

Cleo and Robbi looked at each other. They waited for the girl to tell them more, then started into the park at the 69th Street entrance that was for pedestrians only.

Lilliana touched Cleo's arm. "Um, do you mind if we stick to the roads?" She pointed back over her shoulder to the limo that neither Cleo nor Robbi had noticed was idling along only a few feet behind them. "I'm only allowed to walk places where Carl can drive the car."

Cleo nodded, and the girls went on to 72nd Street where there was an entrance for cars as well as people on foot. They went in and walked south on the winding road that made a circle through the park. It was a strange sight, three girls on the sidewalk at the edge of the road with the gold limo creeping alongside them.

"So, anyway," said Cleo, "what did the note say?"

"They said they'll give Bilbo back if Daddy gives them five hundred thousand dollars. He's supposed to bring the money to a party he's having at his office on Tuesday."

A party? Cleo wondered if this would be another chance to help. "What's this party for? I mean, how many people are coming?"

"Everyone," said Lilliana. "Well, not everyone, but tons of people and, actually, they are coming from all over the world. It's people my dad does business with internationally. Natalie said that the dognappers are probably hoping they'll be able to hide in the crowd."

"Yeah," said Robbi, looking at Cleo. "If there are enough people at the party, I'll bet *anyone* could blend in." She didn't even try to disguise the excitement in her voice.

Cleo chose to ignore her best friend's flagrant hinting. "Well, I'm sure the police must be pretty experienced with cases like this," she said.

"That's just it," said Lilliana. "Daddy's not planning to tell the police anything about it."

Chapter 13

"The note said not to tell anyone or they'd hurt Bilbo," said Lilliana, "so I guess I'm glad he didn't tell that detective. The problem is, I know Daddy doesn't want to hand over the money either. I heard him talking to Natalie last night and he said he's going to try to trap these guys himself." She looked up at Cleo. "What if he goofs it up?"

With a raised eyebrow, Cleo warned her loquacious friend to keep quiet, then took a deep breath. "Listen, Lilliana, I have a . . . friend who might be able to help you. I mean, I can't promise anything, but maybe, if you can tell me everything you know, well, maybe, this friend could help. Maybe." Cleo snuck a peek at Robbi who was doing a thoroughly rotten job of suppressing a grin. "Anyway, do you want me to have her try?"

"How could she help?" asked Lilliana with a doubting look.

"Ah, she, ah, used to be kind of a secret agent. That's all I can say."

"But she's really terrific," blurted out Robbi. "If anybody could help she can. She's awesome."

"Robbi's totally exaggerating," said Cleo quickly. "Anyway, I'm only promising to ask her. She might say no."

"It'd be great if she could help," said Lilliana. "Tell her I'll pay her my allowance for the next thousand years, anything. I'll do whatever it takes to find Bilbo. Please." She was so earnest that Cleo couldn't resist.

"I'll ask," she said.

Lilliana jumped up and down. "Oh, thank you, Cleo. What does your friend need to know?"

"Well, where is your dad supposed to leave the money?" asked Cleo.

The girls learned the exchange of cash for Bilbo was scheduled to happen at 7:00 the evening of the party. Mr. Edsel-Mellon was to put a black briefcase with the money beside a large potted ficus tree just outside of a penthouse conference room.

"They said Bilbo would be left in the same place."

Cleo's mind was racing. She knew she needed a little more information in order to come up with a disguise for Tuesday night. "Lilliana, do you happen to know where we could find a guest list for the party?" asked Cleo in a soft voice.

The girl nodded. "Sure, I think so. Can you come over for a little while?"

When Cleo and Robbi agreed, the little girl turned and gestured. Instantly the gold Rolls pulled up beside the girls and Carl jumped out to open the back door.

"These are my friends, Carl," said Lilliana. "They're going to come to the house for a little while."

The chauffeur didn't say anything, but eyed the teenagers carefully as they climbed into the back seat. He seemed to be memorizing every detail about them.

"This is unbelievable," said Robbi. She was busy checking out the inside of the car that had red velvet upholstered seats and plump pillows thrown around to make the ride as comfortable as possible. There was a cellular phone, and a small refrigerator filled with soft drinks and juices. Somehow it wasn't surprising to see that the car even had a television set, a VCR, and a video game player system.

It was amazing, but riding in the ostentatious vehicle was kind of embarrassing. Through the tinted windows, Cleo could see people they passed staring, shaking their heads, and sometimes even laughing. She suddenly understood why Lilliana had found a ride in a plain old yellow cab to be so liberating.

The journey to the Edsel-Mellon mansion took no time at all in the light Sunday afternoon traffic. Carl let the girls off in front of an impressive brick town house and Lilliana led her friends up the stairs. As the little girl reached the top step, the huge front door opened before Lilliana had even made a motion to knock.

Wow, thought Cleo, *don't the Edsel-Mellons ever*

open their own doors? Between Carl and whoever was behind the massive oak and stained-glass door, Lilliana hadn't even had to touch a handle.

"Miss Lilliana," said a tall, severe-looking butler. He had an unusually high and broad forehead that made him look a little like a balding Frankenstein.

"Mr. Filbert, these are my friends, Cleo and Robbi," said Lilliana as they entered the house.

"Yes, miss," said the large man, speaking very precisely. "I'm sure they are your friends, but unfortunately I don't know them personally. You know the procedure, unless they have some sort of ID, I can't allow them in."

"But they're just kids, like me," protested Lilliana. "I mean, they go to school with JP, how bad could they be?"

That reminded Cleo of something. "Never mind, Lilliana," she said, reaching into her backpack. "Robbi, do you have your subway pass?"

Robbi nodded and both girls pulled out the picture IDs that allowed them to ride the subways and buses free during school hours. "Is this okay?" asked Cleo. "I mean, it says we go to Walton and all."

The butler nodded his head. "Forgive me, young ladies," he said. "But I must follow the rules."

Cleo shrugged. "It's okay," she said. *No wonder Lilliana doesn't have any friends,* she thought. *Who'd want to go through this just to hang out with a friend?*

Robbi muttered something under her breath about how ridiculous this all was, but fortunately no one but

Cleo heard her as the girls entered an impressive foyer.

"Wow," said Cleo after she'd elbowed her friend. A small but old and very beautiful crystal chandelier hung from an arched ceiling, casting shimmering shadows on the parquet floor. On the wall behind a wide stairway leading to the floors above was a huge oil painting of a hunting party at dawn. "This looks like a museum."

"Do you want to see my room?" asked Lilliana shyly.

Cleo and Robbi nodded and followed the girl up to the fifth floor. Along the way were many pieces of turn-of-the-century artwork, both paintings and sculptures, glorious antique furniture, and stately oriental rugs. Everything seemed to say "money," and lots of it.

"Here it is," said Lilliana. Her room looked like something in a photo from a magazine. The wallpaper had a pattern of the tiniest rosebuds in pale pinks and peaches that matched a comforter and canopy on a four-poster bed. A perfect copy in miniature of the canopy bed, complete with comforter, stood against the far wall. The little girl pointed it out. "That's Bilbo's bed," she said sadly.

The room also held a girl-sized vanity and a small dresser. Everything was beautiful, but somehow so perfect that it was hard to imagine someone actually lived here.

"You sure keep it neat," commented Robbi. Her own bedroom was in a continual state of disarray.

"Oh, I make messes," said Lilliana, "but the housekeepers take care of it." She said it nonchalantly as if everyone had maids to clean up after them.

"It's really pretty," said Cleo, meaning it. The room was gorgeous, but she shuddered to think of someone else going through her things, even if it was just to put them away.

Robbi interrupted her thoughts. "So, where's this guest list?" asked the girl who was clearly anxious to get going.

"Oh," said Lilliana, "it's downstairs." She took them to the main floor. "This is my dad's office," she said, pointing toward what looked like a large library, "and this is Elaine's office." She opened the door to an adjoining room. "She's my dad's secretary. Come on in."

"She's not here today, right?" asked Cleo nervously. It was Sunday, but who knew what kind of hours the Edsel-Mellons kept.

"No, I don't think so," said Lilliana. "She's been working a lot lately, but if my dad's not here, she's usually not either. It's probably just JP and us."

"That's it?" asked Robbi. "What about Lurch down there?"

"Mr. Filbert?" asked Lilliana. "Well, I guess if you count the help, there's about four other people in the house, but I'm sure they're all downstairs in the kitchen area. Don't worry, no one will ever bother us in here. JP spends all his time with the computer in his room. He can't think about anything but surfing the Net right now."

It didn't reassure Cleo to know there were so many

people around who might catch them in the office, but she didn't have much choice.

"The list is probably on Elaine's computer," said Lilliana. "I guess we should look there." She went to the desk and turned on the machine. "I don't understand why you want to know who's going though."

Cleo wasn't positive herself yet, and she hesitated before answering. "My friend would probably look through it for possible suspects, that's all," she said. She moved in front of the computer. "Do you mind if I have a look?"

Lilliana moved aside and Cleo, as well as Robbi, crowded in to look at the computer monitor. Cleo clicked the mouse a few times until a list of files came up on the screen. "I just hope she names her files logically," whispered Cleo.

Luckily, Elaine's computer was well organized and straightforward, which made it easy to find a directory named PARTY with files listed by date. Cleo clicked the mouse on the date for Tuesday and a long list of names and addresses popped up on the screen.

Every name had a Y, an N, or a question mark beside it. "Do you mind if I print out this list?" she asked Lilliana. Cleo was worried that she might be committing some sort of crime, but if she had permission it should be okay.

Lilliana nodded and Cleo quickly hit the key to print. As one of the sheets came out a name caught her eye.

It was a family, the Gutapundis from India, and there were two interesting things about their name.

One was that there was an N after it. Apparently, they had declined to attend. The other was that beside the parents' names was another notation: "daughter, Amira, age 18."

When Lilliana wasn't looking, Cleo moved the mouse, clicked onto the name, then typed in a Y over the N. Now the Gutapundis and their daughter were listed as attendees for the Tuesday night bash.

"Okay," demanded Robbi under her breath, "you'd better tell me what you're planning."

Suddenly the door to the office was thrown wide open.

Chapter 14

Mr. Filbert stood there, filling the doorway with his huge frame. "Young ladies, do you have permission to be in here?"

The two teenagers froze with a terrified expression on their faces. Cleo realized that she couldn't have looked guiltier if she had tried.

"Oh, Filbert, go away," said Lilliana, dismissing the man like she would shoo off a gnat.

"Yes, miss," said Filbert and he sheepishly closed the door.

The two Walton girls breathed a deep sigh of relief.

"He's just a great big busybody," said Lilliana.

But this had been a close call for Cleo and Robbi and they decided they'd better get out before someone else caught them in the secretary's office.

"I think we should get home," said Cleo, "but thanks. I'm sure this will help my friend. Are you going to be at the party?"

Lilliana shook her head. "They think I'll be too nervous so I have to stay home, but Daddy promised to call as soon as they have Bilbo. I'll call you right after, okay?"

Cleo nodded, then she and Robbi moved toward the door. They weren't anxious to run into Mr. Filbert again, and sure enough, the man was waiting at the bottom of the stairs.

"Shall I call the car around?" he asked Lilliana.

"Yes, please," she said, then looked at Cleo and Robbi. "You are going to ride home with Carl, aren't you?"

Not wanting to be impolite, the girls accepted only to regret the decision as soon as they got into the "glitter machine" as Robbi had already dubbed the car. They were dying to discuss the upcoming party, but it was impossible with the chauffeur glaring at them in the rearview mirror like they were a pair of escaped convicts. The two friends endured the ride to the West Side in silence, too uncomfortable even to make casual chitchat.

It wasn't until they were sitting in Cleo's bedroom that they felt like they could talk. "Robbi, I'm going to be at that party," said Cleo. She picked up Phoebe. "Am I crazy?"

"Three hundred percent," said Robbi, "but it's great. I mean, the police won't be there so it won't be like you're obstructing justice or anything."

"Yeah, well, one wrong move and it could be curtains for Bilbo," said Cleo. "I mean, it's actually a life or death situation this time. You don't think we should let the adults handle this whole thing, do you?"

"No way," said Robbi. "Grown-ups *think* they know everything, but look, even on TV, something always goes wrong on these ransom drops. Both sides come in expecting the other side to pull some sort of double cross. You'll have an advantage because no one will even know you're there. I'm sure you'll be able to catch whoever took Bilbo."

As it often did, Robbi's "logic" left Cleo feeling even more filled with doubt, but one thing she had said actually did make sense, in a twisted sort of way. Since no one would know Cleo was there, she'd have a definite advantage, both to observe and to ask questions. Even if she wasn't able to apprehend the culprit, she might at least be able to give the police a good description. She gave her rabbit a scratch behind the ears and set her down.

"It's a good thing a person can't outgrow a sari."

It felt like a couple of eternities had gone by before the last bell of the day rang on Tuesday, but Cleo had used the time well. She'd spent Monday after school at the library, researching what Indian women looked like, getting photocopies of the way they wrapped their saris and applied their makeup. She knew it was going to take a lot of time to get into this disguise, so as soon as Cleo was out the gates she started jogging and didn't let up until she was at her front door.

"Hi, Nortrud," she said as she whizzed through the kitchen. "I'm just dropping off my books, then I'm going to Robbi's." She sniffed the air that was scented with rosemary chicken. "And did you remember that I said I'm going to have dinner with the Richardses?" Cleo could pretty much count on Nortrud to forget anything.

"Oh, my," said the housekeeper. "Well, now, I guess it did slip my mind. Are you sure Robbi doesn't want to join you here?"

Cleo shook her head. Eating at Robbi's was the perfect excuse for being out of the house during the hours of the party tonight. "Sorry, Nortrud, but I'm sure your chicken will still taste great tomorrow. Listen, I gotta go, okay?"

She rushed to her bedroom and dropped her backpack on the desk. Then she pulled her makeup case from the closet and stuffed a large square of fabric, flat sandals, and a lycra midriff top into her black overnight bag. Before she left the room, she stood in front of the full-length mirror. *Good luck,* she told her reflection. She knew she was going to need it.

The Richardses lived on West 86th Street between Riverside Drive and West End Avenue in an old brownstone that Robbi's father, an architect, was renovating in his spare time. Robbi swore that the work on the house was progressing but one part of the brownstone or another always seemed to be half demolished and it was impossible to really tell. Cleo, Robbi, and Alyssa had taken bets on when the place would be finished and Cleo's guess was sometime near the middle of the next century.

The girls went up to the fourth floor where Robbi and her older brother, Carver, had their bedrooms. In addition, there were two other rooms that someday would be guest bedrooms, but at present were only empty shells without finished walls or ceilings.

"Now you're sure we're alone?" Cleo asked. The girls had gone to the Richards home to escape Nortrud's watchful eye, but Cleo knew it would be even worse if Robbi's mother or brother saw her disguising herself.

"I told you, Mom's at an audition and Carver's at school working on the newspaper," said Robbi. "Now relax."

"Yeah, right." Cleo started by sweeping her arm across Robbi's bed to push away the stack of clothes and books her friend always had piled on top. Once the area was semicleared, Cleo took out the photocopies from the library and laid them on the bed, then she went to work.

First she pulled her hair back. It was always one of the hardest things for Cleo to get right. Grabbing her hairbrush she attacked the black mass on her head, trying to twist it into a low bun.

"Not," said Robbi, who'd plopped herself down to watch. "The back of your head looks like a mega furball."

Cleo picked up the hand mirror from her makeup case and checked the rear view of her head. Robbi was right. Her hair looked awful. "By the time I get this even close, the party will be over," she lamented.

"What are you talking about?" said Robbi, scrambling to her feet. "Sit down." She put her hands on Cleo's shoulders and forced her to sit. "Let an expert take care of the situation."

She quickly undid Cleo's handiwork, then started brushing the black hair back.

"Hey, watch it," cried Cleo. "You're giving me whiplash." Her friend was brushing with far too much enthusiasm.

"Sorry," apologized Robbi. She pulled the hair back into a low ponytail, then went around front to look at Cleo. "Not bad, but I think you definitely need some superhold gel. Getting those bangs down is going to take a hammer."

Cleo's eyes opened wide.

"Only kidding." Robbi slopped a generous amount of goop into her hand, then slicked back Cleo's hair so it was smooth and amazingly neat. Next she twisted the ponytail into a bun and quickly pinned it in place. A hairnet over the bun tamed the stray hairs into a neat knot.

"That's great, Rob," said Cleo. She'd had doubts about her friend being able to pull it off, but the bun was perfect.

Time for makeup. Cleo took out two shades of dark foundation from the cherrywood box. She needed the heaviness of one shade to cover her own pale skin, but the makeup was a little too dark so she toned it down by mixing in some of a peachier tint. Next she applied her custom-made color to her face with a small wedge-shaped sponge until her complexion was perfectly smooth and many shades darker than her own alabaster. Cleo made sure to apply the color to her neck and asked Robbi to check around the nape of her neck as well as inside and behind her ears.

She studied the pictures from *National Geographic* of women from New Delhi, and copied the black kohl pencil outlining onto her eyes, then added a light coat of black mascara. A dark rose lipstick looked natural and also emphasized her full lips. After donning a pair of gold hoop earrings, Cleo decided she would pass, at least from the neck up.

Now she slipped into her short-sleeved midriff top, then whisked the large square of silk fabric out of her bag. Her uncle Lionel had brought it back two years ago from one of his expeditions to the Far East and though Cleo had always admired the sari, she had never been quite sure what she'd do with it. Never in a million years did she think she'd have an occasion to actually wear it.

She unfolded the brilliant green silk with its gold embroidered edge and stared. "How in the world are we going to get this to look right?"

Half an hour later, with the aid of many safety pins, the two girls had managed to wrap the sari into an outfit that very closely resembled the photos in *National Geographic*. "It'll have to do," declared Cleo. "If only this thing had come with instructions."

The last thing she had to do was to make up her arms, hands, and feet. She mixed some special powder she'd gotten at the theatrical makeup store until it closely matched the shade of her face. Then she had Robbi sponge it on every bit of exposed skin, from her arms to the tips of her fingers, to her stomach, even her toes. The final touch was putting on a pair of gold sandals.

"So, my good friend," she said, adopting a hint of the guttural Indian accent she heard so often from the cabdrivers in the city, "how are you thinking that I am looking this fine day?"

Robbi started giggling. "That's great," she said. "You look like you should be sitting outside the Taj Mahal." She glanced at her watch. "Oh, hey, it's almost six. You'd better get going."

Cleo picked up a gold sweater and a small evening bag, then hurried to the street. She caught a cab easily and to her relief, the driver wasn't Indian. She might be able to fool Robbi with her accent, but Cleo wasn't so sure about fooling someone from India. She gave the driver directions to the Edsel-Mellon Building in midtown and pulled out her compact to check her makeup again.

In Manhattan during the week, whether it was rush hour or not, traffic always seemed to be impossible and the ride took longer than Cleo had anticipated. By the time she reached the skyscraper, she was just as nervous about being late as she was about pulling off her masquerade.

The Edsel-Mellon Building was a dark steel and glass monolith designed with a forced perspective, smaller at the top than the bottom, that made the structure seem even taller and grander than it was. Cleo paid the cabdriver, then stepped sedately into the impressive lobby. She walked across slick dark gray marble floors that made Cleo glad that she hadn't opted to wear any sort of heels. It would be pretty tough to get into the party inconspicuously after making a skidding grand entrance through the building.

It was impossible to miss the EDSEL-MELLON PARTY sign near the bank of elevators in the center of the lobby. Beside the sign stood a young man in a tuxedo with a clipboard who was checking people off a list.

"This is it," Undercover Cleo whispered to herself. She put a hand to her hair to make sure it was all still in place, then took leisurely steps toward the man.

"Yes?" he said. He sounded monumentally bored.

"Excuse me, sir," said Undercover Cleo, "I am to meet my family for the party that Mr. Edsel-Mellon is giving this evening. My name is Amira Gutapundi. Would you be able to tell me if indeed they have arrived?" She kept her voice pitched low and was careful with her accent.

"Guta-what?" asked the man.

"Gutapundi, Amira," she said, then spelled it out. *Oh, no*, she thought in a sudden panic, *what if someone caught the switch I made on the computer list.* She braced herself for the worst, but the young man found her name a second later.

"Here it is," he said. "No, your parents haven't arrived yet." He looked over the clipboard and scrutinized the girl, then checked off her name. "You can go ahead if you want. I'll send them up when they get here."

"Amira" let the tiniest of smiles escape. "Thank you so very much, sir."

"But please, first, would you mind stepping through this way?" The man indicated a metal-detecting entrance gate, just like the one at *Natalie's Dream*. "Sorry about the inconvenience but I'm sure you can understand why."

The girl nodded and obliged and after she had passed through without setting off the machine, the young man pushed the button to the elevator nearest him. When it opened he held the door for Undercover Cleo, then reached in, inserted a key, and pushed PH. The doors closed and "Amira" was catapulted upward on an "express" ride to the penthouse.

Only seconds later the girl stepped out into a crowded but mellow party. Elaine, the social secretary, looking perfectly turned out in a navy suit with a simple cream shell top, stood off to the side, welcoming guests as they emerged from the elevators.

The panic Cleo felt was like a needle stuck into her heart. Knowing the secretary had been the one to take the RSVPs, the girl was sure her gig was up. Anyone as meticulous as Elaine seemed to be would surely remember that the Gutapundis had declined the invitation this evening.

Cleo forced herself to breathe normally and hoped she wasn't sweating when things got worse. Her legs just about went out from under her as Mr. Edsel-Mellon himself stepped directly toward her.

Chapter 15

"You must be Amira," he said, offering her his hand. "I'm sure you don't remember me, but I'd recognize your mother's eyes anywhere. You've certainly grown up into a beautiful young woman."

Undercover Cleo smiled graciously. "You are too kind," she said.

"Are your parents here this evening?" Mr. Edsel-Mellon ushered the girl in past the secretary.

"Not yet," said "Amira," relieved to have gotten past yet one more checkpoint, "but they will be along quite soon I am sure."

"Glad to hear that," said Mr. Edsel-Mellon, "I'm looking forward to seeing them." His eyes wandered off beyond Undercover Cleo to the elevator doors opening behind her. "Good of you to join us, too," he said. "Will you excuse me?" As he stepped away to greet a group of newcomers, the girl exhaled and shook her head. That had taken her totally by surprise.

She picked up a glass of soda and cruised through the party, trying to appear relaxed at the same time that she searched for the potted ficus tree where the exchange was to take place. There were less than twenty minutes until the switch was scheduled to go down. She moved from room to room, making careful observations of the other guests and trying to commit their faces to memory. Undercover Cleo knew that any one of these people could be involved in the dognapping.

A roving photographer snapped pictures of the clusters of people and nervously the teen detective kept her distance as she made her investigation. The problem was, she didn't know who she was looking for. As her eyes wandered the room, it was almost irritating to note that everyone seemed to belong at the party. In fact, it appeared that she was the only one who was not engaged in conversation. *I'm probably the most suspicious person here,* she realized, but she also knew it would be risky to stop and talk with anyone. She couldn't afford to miss the 7:00 drop.

Just then, Cleo spotted the ficus plant. Looking closely at the wall near it, she noticed an outline of a set of double doors—obviously the entrance to the conference room in this modern-styled building. She took a step toward the area, intending to find a place where she could observe the exchange, when a familiar voice stopped her cold.

"Hi, I'm JP."

Undercover Cleo whirled to see JP Edsel-Mellon looking up at her and smiling broadly. *Tell me this isn't happening,* she thought. *He's going to recognize me.*

Amazingly, the boy didn't seem to know her at all. "What's your name?" he asked.

Cleo was relieved but realized she was running out of time. "I'm Amira Gutapundi," she said without smiling. No point in being friendly. She needed to make this conversation as brief as possible.

"The Gutapundis?" said JP. "Wow, your family practically owns New Delhi."

Great, thought Cleo. She knew the one thing that would impress the boy was money and apparently her "family" had plenty of it.

"Tell me, is that story about your great-grandmother true?" asked the boy. "You know, the one about her bathtub being set with rubies so the water would always be the perfect color of pink?"

Undercover Cleo bit her tongue and tried to keep her composure. It sounded like a ridiculous fairy tale, but how would she know? "I don't like to talk about my family," she said finally.

To her surprise, this only seemed to add to JP's fascination with "Amira."

"Well, I've heard the story's true," he said.

He seemed mesmerized by her. Cleo could see it in his eyes, in the way he smiled so goofily at her, and she racked her brain for a way to extricate herself from the conversation. It was getting close to seven.

"I'm sorry," she said, "but do you have the time? I'm supposed to meet my boyfriend in a few minutes."

The boy's face fell and for a moment Cleo felt bad, but only for a moment. He extended his arm and checked a gold Rolex on his wrist. "It's five to seven. I'll walk you to the elevator."

This had to be a nightmare. Cleo was desperate now. With so little time left, she knew she had to do something drastic to get rid of the boy or all of her work on this disguise would be wasted. She started to walk in the direction of the elevators, then stumbled, carefully splashing the remains of her soda on JP's tux shirt.

"Oh, dear," she exclaimed. "I'm so very, very sorry."

JP looked as if he was going to cry and without a word he turned and hurried off toward the rest rooms, leaving Undercover Cleo free to glide calmly to the vicinity of the ficus.

There were several groups of people conversing near the drop point, so it was easy for Undercover Cleo to drift in a wide circle around the edge of the room while keeping a sharp eye on the tree. As she watched, Mr. Edsel-Mellon casually walked over to the ficus and set a black briefcase at the base of the planter. He glanced around, then left the room. The girl's heartbeat quickened.

Suddenly she realized she hadn't really thought out the situation. What should she do? Should she yell out or try to follow the dognapper? Unless it was someone like the elderly woman, Cleo wasn't going to be able to apprehend the culprit. For a moment the teen went light-headed with fear and had to lean back against the wall to steady herself.

Just then, the young man who had admitted her into the party came out of the elevator and went straight toward the ficus plant. Cleo inhaled sharply when she saw he was holding a pet carrying case in his right hand. To her surprise, the man didn't appear nervous or concerned in the least. He actually smiled and looked relieved when he saw the briefcase under the tree.

Cleo stood up, her dizziness gone, watching the man as he went to the planter, set down the pet carrying case, then picked up the black briefcase. A moment later he turned to head back to the elevators.

I've got to stop him, thought Cleo, but before she could take a step, four men and two women rushed at the young party attendant, coming at him from all different directions. In moments they had surrounded the man.

"Hey, what's going on?" he cried. "Let me go!" He struggled to get free, but the guards easily pinned his hands behind his back and handcuffed him.

Good thing I didn't get in the way of that, thought Cleo.

The almost-hidden doors that led to the conference room behind the ficus tree slid open and to the girl's surprise, Detective Milton burst out. As the teen stood there nearly paralyzed, Herbert Edsel-Mellon strode into the midst of the melee, obviously not surprised by the appearance of the police.

He must have called Detective Milton after all, Cleo concluded. She also couldn't help having the feeling that somehow they had managed to get the wrong guy.

Shaking herself out of her stupor and moving at a pace she thought of as "casually rushing," she made her way as close to the action as she dared. Detective Milton was reading the man his rights as Mr. Edsel-Mellon stood by looking exceptionally pleased with himself.

"Look," shouted the young man, "I don't know what's going on. Some guy gave me a hundred bucks to swap that kennel for the black briefcase." He now appeared to be hyperventilating.

"Come on, son," said Todd Milton, "don't tell me you don't know anything about the Edsel-Mellons' dog being snatched."

"Well, of course, but"—the young man's face suddenly registered total shock—"you mean, the dog's in there? So the briefcase is filled with . . . money? Oh, mama."

To Cleo, his shock seemed sincere.

"That's right," said Detective Milton. "I'll be straight: buddy, it's lookin' really bad for you. You might as well spill your guts, and right now." The words were those of a tough street-smart police officer, but hearing them uttered in Todd Milton's high quivering tenor caused Cleo to bite her tongue to keep from giggling.

A uniformed policeman walked up holding the pet carrier. "Is this what you wanted, sir?" he asked Mr. Edsel-Mellon.

Lilliana's father took the case and set it on the ground. "Lot of trouble for a dog," he mumbled. He opened the case, and to everyone's surprise there was nothing inside but a small sack of rice and a stuffed dog. "What the . . . ?"

"Where's the animal?" Detective Milton asked the young attendant. "Speak up and it'll go easier for you."

"I'm telling you, I don't know a thing," said the man. "This guy, short stocky man with a tan, came up to me downstairs . . ."

As soon as he said the word "downstairs," Cleo was off, moving rapidly for the elevators. Someone must be waiting in the lobby for this young man to bring him the briefcase of money. The girl pushed the button for the elevator to the main floor.

Hadn't Robbi said that one side or the other was always ready for a setup in a ransom situation? It looked like this time, both sides had "cheated." Maybe, if Undercover Cleo hurried, she could catch a glimpse of the real dognapper.

Where is that elevator? she thought, tapping her foot impatiently. Finally it appeared, and she quickly stepped into the car. She put her hand out to push the button for the lobby when Detective Milton looked in her direction and waved frantically. He had just figured it out.

"Hold that car!" he yelled.

"Going down! Going down!" yelled another man, as the entire group, including Detective Milton, rushed toward her.

She had a moment of indecision, then smiled and nodded toward the approaching men. She made a motion, pretending to push the OPEN button, but in actuality she punched CLOSE several times and was relieved to see the doors slide shut.

Cleo had made a calculated decision. The officers were all wearing suits—if they burst out of the elevator downstairs, they would be sure to scare off any dognapper. Undercover Cleo would have a better chance of spotting the culprit on her own, so she left the police to catch the next elevator car. By the time they got to the lobby, she would be able to point out the suspect.

As the car shot downward, Cleo could hear the officers yelling and banging on the doors. Knowing she'd only have seconds before the police arrived, the teen detective readied herself to scan the lobby for the dognapper.

What was the description the young assistant gave? A short, stocky man with a tan, that's it, she thought as her eyes darted around the main floor. He had to be here, since there was no reason for him to suspect anything had gone wrong yet. She wondered if the dognapper was waiting outside and had just started off in the direction of the huge glass doors when Detective Milton and his team burst out from the next elevator. Guns drawn, the officers made a spectacle of themselves as they spun around looking for their suspect.

The group moved to block off the front exit and began questioning everyone on the floor. Cleo knew it was just a matter of time before they got to her and there was no way she was going to stand around answering questions about a party she'd just crashed. Stepping back, her eyes searched for an alternate way out.

A sudden movement caught her attention as she inched her way past the elevators. Her eyes were still adjusting to the dimly lit lobby when she saw a dark man in a corner in the shadow of a huge column slip into a lobby side exit.

Oh, my gosh, she thought. *It's him.* Most of the policemen were at the far end of the lobby, still checking everyone leaving the building, and since she knew from experience that Todd Milton was neither the fastest nor the most graceful man on his feet, Cleo decided it was up to her.

The teen detective yanked up the skirt of her sari and dashed after the suspect. With total disregard for a sign that read EMERGENCY EXIT ONLY, the man rammed the door open and shot out. An obnoxiously loud alarm went off and Cleo could hear shouts behind her. Without even looking, she knew the police would be behind her in close pursuit and if she didn't hurry, she knew the man would get away.

"W-h-o-a!" A yell was followed by four loud whomps.

Undercover Cleo spun to see what had happened—

Detective Milton and three of his cohorts were on their rumps, sliding across the ice-slick marble floor. While they were pulling each other down, trying to get back on their feet, "Amira" dashed after the short man who'd just disappeared through the exit.

Luckily, the stocky suspect was no athlete and it wasn't too hard for Cleo to keep up with him, even wearing her unlikely running outfit. She chased him out the door into the street and down 40th Street where he turned into a dark alley. Hearing the growl of a low-pitched engine, she slowed down and instead of rushing recklessly into the shadowy narrow space, the girl only peeked around the corner.

Climbing into the passenger seat of a beat-up gray van was the man she had been chasing. Seconds later, the vehicle came hurtling toward Cleo on its way to the street.

"Amira" plastered herself back against the brick wall as the van careened directly toward her. She caught only a glimpse of the driver, a woman with an Irish walking cap pulled low over her face who turned the wheel wildly. As the speeding machine roared past the terrified girl, Cleo's eyes were riveted to one striking detail: a large-faced watch with a grimy leather strap on the woman's left wrist.

Chapter 16

Cleo watched as Bilbo's abductors turned onto Park Avenue, their taillights growing smaller in the distance. *I'm not going to let this chase end here*, she thought to herself. After the foul-up in the Edsel-Mellon Building, there might not be much time left for the little dog.

Running out into the street, Cleo raised a long arm and quickly flagged a passing cab headed downtown. Three drivers saw the girl at the same time, and as often happened in New York City, the taxi that was farthest away cut in front of the other two cars as well as across two lanes of traffic before screeching and skidding to a stop in front of "Amira."

"Yes, miss," said the driver who was, to Undercover Cleo's dismay, an East Indian.

Knowing this was no time to be choosy, the girl

clambered into the back seat and pointed to the gray vehicle zipping from lane to lane. "Follow that van," she commanded.

The cabdriver, a thin, clean-shaven, and very dark-skinned man, nodded and zoomed off. "Oh, very certainly, miss. Your wish is my command."

Cleo grabbed the handle on the door frame as the cab took off and she was thrown back in her seat. In a matter of seconds she was slammed forward and backward several times and when she checked the driver's taxi license, posted over the glove compartment, she wasn't happy to see the man had been granted it only the week before. Great.

"Miss, forgive me, but I must tell you, you are very, very, *very* beautiful," said the driver. "It is not often I have the honor of escorting such a lovely countryman of mine around this great city."

She gave him a rather sick smile. "That's nice," she said. *He can't possibly think I'm Indian, because I haven't been using the accent*, she thought. *He probably thinks I was raised in this country.*

"I see that you are not yet married, miss," said the man as he tried to catch "Amira's" eye in the rearview mirror.

Cleo was mortified. She had, of course, left off the red mark on her forehead that signified a married woman. What was going on here? Was this man interested in her? He had to be at least thirty-five.

"Uh, no, sir," she stammered. "I guess I'm not married."

She turned her focus to the van in front of her that

seemed to be gaining ground. "Excuse me, but do you think you could hurry just a little bit more? It's really important that I find out where those people are going."

The driver nodded his head and floored the gas. The cab surged just as a tire dipped into one of New York's infamous potholes, sending the rear end of the car bouncing all over the street. Cleo flew up in the air and banged her head on the ceiling of the cab.

"Hey," she cried. "I want to catch the van, but I'd like to still be alive when I do."

"So sorry, miss," said the driver. He was looking worriedly into the rearview mirror. "Are you quite all right? Are you in need of any assistance?"

"I'm fine," answered Cleo, "but please, just watch where you're going." They were picking up speed and gaining on the van and she closed her eyes as the taxi narrowly missed a limo, then reopened them so as not to lose sight of the fleeing suspects. "Look, they're turning off up ahead." The van had just made a left turn heading east.

"Have no fears, miss," said the man, "I swear to you that I, Rajbhushan Kairali, shall catch this vehicle for you or die trying."

Cleo was trying to decide whether she liked this answer or not as the cab reeled around the corner onto 28th Street, the squeal of the tires scaring her half to death. Fortunately, she was rewarded by the sight of the battered gray van up ahead, slipping in front of a large moving truck. At least they hadn't lost the vehicle yet.

"This is quite exciting, is it not?" asked Rajbhushan with a big grin on his face. "Just like in the cinema. You are fortunate that I am such a brave cabdriver."

Then something awful happened. The mover's truck slowed to a halt on the narrow crosstown street, then the hazard lights began blinking. As Cleo watched, the driver jumped out and began to undo the locks on the back doors while at the same time, another man stepped out and motioned for the cars, including Cleo's taxi, to back up out of the street.

"Oh, dear," said the driver. "I'm afraid we must find another route to chase your gray van." It was obvious that the movers were planning to unload their huge vehicle right where it was stopped.

Cleo pounded her fist into the seat of the cab as the driver backed up, then sped off, going around the block in hopes of somehow catching up to the gray van. The Indian man was eager to please his beautiful passenger and took the cab across 26th Street and onto Lexington Avenue. When they got back to 28th Street, they were amazed to see the van was still heading east.

"That's incredible," said Cleo. She focused all her attention on the van, willing the driver not to lose the suspects again. Suddenly the gray vehicle sped up and started darting in and out of traffic.

"I believe they are on to us," said the driver. He suddenly seemed very nervous, but he accelerated just the same.

They managed to stay on the dognappers' tail

around a few corners, then abruptly the gray van vanished.

Cleo couldn't believe it. She'd been so close. "Just keep driving for a little while," she ordered, but the van was nowhere in sight. After turning a few more corners, she reluctantly decided to call off the chase.

"I guess we lost them," she said, slumping down in her seat. "Please take me to . . ."

"Oh, no, miss! Big trouble," cried Rajbhushan. He sounded frightened, causing Cleo to look up.

The man was staring wide-eyed into his rearview mirror, and this time he wasn't looking at "Amira." The teen whirled and looked out the back window to see the gray van bearing down on the taxi.

Chapter 17

"Now how did they get behind us?" asked Cleo.

"Miss," said the man, "this is no accident. I have made several turns. Those people are definitely following us now." The driver's bravery had suddenly disappeared.

"Can you lose them?"

It was amazing to watch how much faster Rajbhushan could drive the cab now that he was the one being pursued, but no matter what he did, the van stayed right behind them. Cleo couldn't fathom why they would be following her, but whatever the reason, it wasn't good.

"Please, miss," begged the cabdriver who now had sweat streaming down his face, although it wasn't very warm in the cab, "it is now time for my break. If only you would kindly step out of my cab, I will not even ask for you to give me a tip."

Sensing the man was on the verge of panic, Cleo made a concerted effort to stay calm. She knew she didn't have long before the driver did something drastic, and she did not intend to be dumped on the sidewalk facing the occupants of the menacing van. She glued her face to the side window to check the street signs. Where was she?

Third Avenue and Tenth Street. Cleo's mind was racing. "Sir," she said, "if you take me to the subway station at Union Square, I'll get out." It was only a few blocks away and she was familiar with the station because it was at one end of the Village.

"Okay, yes, very good," said the man, wiping his brow and rapidly nodding his head. In minutes they had reached the station with the van still a car's length behind them. Cleo saw the meter read over eight dollars and she shoved a ten-dollar bill at the man before dashing out the door of the taxi. With the skirt of her sari wadded up in one hand, the teenager sprinted down the stairs of the subway entrance into the darkness below.

She heard a scream of brakes as the van skidded to a halt. The banging of a metal door told her that at least one of the suspects must have gotten out and was probably coming after her, but she didn't dare even glance over her shoulder as she raced down.

This particular station was a stop for several different subway lines and rather than getting on the first train, the teen launched herself down the steps to the lowest level and through a maze of tunnels until she reached the platform for the L train.

Fumbling for her MetroCard, Cleo swiped it in the turnstile, then hurried through. She felt her prayers were answered when a train pulled into the station and she hopped nervously from foot to foot until the doors opened.

The teen boarded at the head of the train, then turned to look behind her. To her horror, the short stocky man had been following her and was digging in his pockets for a fare card or token.

Cleo held her breath, hoping the doors would close and the train would leave before the man found a token, but when the conductor looked out his window to check for last-minute stragglers, the stocky man leapt over the turnstile and flung himself toward the train. Just as the doors closed, she saw the dognapper squeeze onto the last car.

Now I'm really stuck, thought Cleo. The man had to be rushing toward her from car to car as the train barreled west. It would only be a matter of seconds before he caught up to her and this time she had nowhere else to run. The subway she'd hoped would be her means of escape had turned into her trap.

An added problem was the bright green and gold sari she had wrapped around her waist and bunched up around her thighs. There was no way she would ever fade into a crowd inconspicuously wearing this outfit.

The next station was only a long block and a half from where she had got on, and the ride took less than two minutes. Cleo braced herself for a sprint, gathering her skirt in her fists. When the doors opened, the girl bolted for the stairs.

Because the dognapping suspect had made it to the middle of the train, he had to fight his way through a small crowd of people who were waiting to board. It was the break Undercover Cleo needed. Her long legs took her quickly to the stairs, but as a group of people came down into the station toward her, she ducked and walked behind them until she reached the token booth. "Amira" squeezed herself between the rear of the booth and the wall, then, squatting down, she watched as the culprit rushed past her and out of the station.

The moment he was out of sight, the teen detective hurried back toward the train. She swiped her card once more through the turnstile slot, then ran to the door of the nearest car.

She was sure she was safe until a beat later the dognapper came rushing down the stairs, spotted her, and galloped toward the waiting train. Undercover Cleo reached the train moments before the doors closed. She hurled herself inside and turned to see if the man would also manage to get in.

Only his hand made it. As "Amira" and the other passengers watched, the rubber door moldings closed around his wrist, and the fingers of a meaty hand spread wide. The teen detective couldn't help noticing several scratches and a row of heavy calluses on his palm just below his fingers.

Knowing the doors would open once again to allow the man to free his hand, the girl dashed to the middle of the car. When the conductor released the door lock, the man jammed his way into the train. At the very same moment Cleo stepped out from the center doors of the car back onto the platform. From here, the teen detective watched the stocky man shaking his fists at her through the subway car window as the train whisked him away to the next stop.

Chapter 18

It had been unnervingly close, and Cleo wasn't convinced the man wouldn't do something really nuts like jump off and run back along the tracks to find her. She hurriedly went through the station and up the stairs to the street. A minute later she was flagging down her third taxi of the evening.

Cleo was relieved to see that while this driver was also from India, he had a picture of a woman and two young children on his sun visor. "Just go around the block," she said, panting to catch her breath.

The man nodded and without any questions made a right turn. "As you wish, miss," he said. She was very thankful that he was not the talkative type.

Cleo leaned into the corner of the seat trying to stay as invisible as possible from outside. After they'd gone around a few corners, she ventured a peek out the back window. The gray van was nowhere in sight.

Satisfied she was no longer being followed, the girl relaxed and gave Robbi's address to the man. It was a great feeling to be heading for the Upper West Side.

As she cleaned off her makeup and changed back into her own jeans and baggy shirt, Cleo filled her friend in on the adventure. Before putting on her shoes, she gingerly checked her feet. Giant blisters had popped up where the straps of the sandals had worked their way into her skin.

"I'll get you some Band-Aids," said Robbi. "Next time, you'd better take along some running shoes."

She sped out of the room, leaving Cleo by herself thinking, *Next time?* After tonight's escapade, she was beginning to wonder if she wasn't getting too deep into Undercover Cleo. Her "covert operations" were costing her a lot of time and a lot of money, but more importantly, they had suddenly turned dangerous.

On the other hand, she had managed to pick up quite a few clues. She now had a pair of suspects. One was a tanned stocky man with scratches and calluses on his hands and the other, a woman who just might have been the bent-over elderly lady who walked off *Natalie's Dream* possibly carrying Bilbo. Either that or it was a complete coincidence that the women were wearing the same oversized and grungy watch. Plus there was a battered gray van, maybe she could have it . . .

"Oh, no," cried Cleo. She slapped herself on the forehead, then fell back onto Robbi's bed.

"What's up?" asked her friend as she handed Cleo the box of bandages.

"I'm so stupid, I didn't get the license plate of the van."

"Cleo," scolded Robbi, "that's the first thing you're supposed to do. If you watched more police shows on TV you'd know that." Robbi was the ultimate TV law and crime show buff.

"Yeah, I know. It's just that I was scared and all I thought of was catching up with the guy . . . or running away."

Cleo was still angry with herself when she got back to her building on Central Park West. Apparently, she just wasn't cut out for the detective business. She let herself into the empty apartment and went straight to her room. The girl dropped her black overnight bag on the floor of her closet, then carefully packed up her makeup case. She wouldn't be needing this anytime soon.

The one thing she regretted was telling Lilliana that a "friend" would try to help. Cleo knew she could make an anonymous call to Detective Milton, leaving the clues she'd managed to gather, but she had really wanted to do more to help get Bilbo home.

The girl looked over at her desk and sighed. It wouldn't be the worst idea in the world for her to get some of her math out of the way. She had just opened her book when the phone rang.

It was Lilliana. "Oh, Cleo, you'll never believe what happened." She ran down the whole fiasco for Cleo, who felt a sickening lump develop in her stomach. It only got worse as Lilliana continued. "Did you by any chance tell your friend about all this?" asked the little girl. "Remember, you said you knew someone who might be able to help? I really need her."

Cleo gulped. "Uh, look, Lilliana, I did talk to my friend, but you know, she's like kind of busy right now. She said she wished she could help, but, um, she just can't. I'm sorry." Cleo shut her eyes tightly and yanked at her hair. It was awful having to lie, especially to a friend, but her mind was made up.

"Oh," said Lilliana. "I see." The disappointment came across strong and clear, even over the phone. "Well, anyway, we got faxed another picture of Bilbo tonight. He's still alive."

Cleo nearly dropped the phone. "What? You got a picture tonight?"

"Yeah. The lady dognapper called again, and I heard she was pretty upset, but she said she'd give us one more chance tomorrow. Daddy's supposed to meet someone in the middle of the George Washington Bridge at 6:30 on a pull-off on the westbound upper deck. He's supposed to bring a bag with the money and the lady said if there was any funny business, that would be it for Bilbo. Then she sent us a picture of him sitting on a copy of today's *Times*."

"Well, I'm sure everything will go fine this time," Cleo managed to say.

"It better," said Lilliana. "Bilbo looks awfully droopy, and I'm really worried about him." She started to cry. "Daddy says he wants me to get my dog back, but the police told him that even if he does pay, we may not get Bilbo back. The dognappers might keep him and ask for even more money." She stopped a moment to sniffle. "Listen, I've got to go, but I told you I'd call, and, well, I just thought you'd want to know what happened." She hung up the phone before Cleo could say good-bye, but not soon enough that the teen detective couldn't hear the little girl's heart-wrenching sobs.

Cleo put down the receiver and slowly walked back to her bedroom. She curled up in her cuddy chair and pulled her favorite blanket around herself. *I can't believe this,* she thought. *I just made up my mind to get out of the undercover spy business.* The thing was, Lilliana really needed her.

Cleo sighed. It seemed like the older she got, the more complicated her decisions became. There was always one more "but."

The fact that the dognappers called so soon after the disaster at the Edsel-Mellon party to make another appointment meant they were anxious for the exchange to take place, or at least for money to change hands. Cleo suddenly became outraged that these people had stolen a poor helpless animal, and she realized that even if the exchange took place without a hitch tomorrow, she wanted these people to pay for what they had done.

She unwound her legs and stood up. For better or worse, she'd rethought her decision to quit being Undercover Cleo. The girl went to the kitchen and picked up the phone and called her best friend. "So, Rob," she said, "how do you feel about cutting classes tomorrow?"

Chapter 19

Robbi wasn't exactly enthusiastic about the idea of missing a whole day at Walton. Though Cleo sometimes thought that Robbi did and said things just to be different from everyone else, she knew her quirky friend well enough to know that she really did like going to classes.

"It's for a good cause, Rob," said Cleo. "And it'll definitely be an adventure." When she explained what she intended to do, she knew that Robbi was tempted and it didn't take much more persuasion before Cleo's friend was actually excited over the plans.

The next day, as usual, both girls left their respective homes for school, but instead of meeting up with one another in homeroom, Cleo walked to the subway station at 72nd Street and Central Park West where she caught the uptown C train. At 86th Street, she peeked her head out and, as expected, did not see her friend waiting on the platform.

The tall teen got off the train and paced back and forth until Robbi finally showed up fifteen minutes late. Together, the girls rode up to 175th Street, near the George Washington Bridge, one of the major arteries into Manhattan from New Jersey and points west.

Cleo and Robbi walked to Riverside Park and found themselves a comfortable, cozy, and out-of-the-way niche overlooking the magnificent bridge. It was unlikely, but still possible, that a police officer or two might be patrolling the park and it would be pretty difficult to find Bilbo if they got grounded for playing hooky.

Both girls had brought along a backpack, but today, they weren't full of schoolbooks. Cleo had brought her father's binoculars and Robbi had borrowed her dad's telescope and once they were safely ensconced in the branches of a large oak tree, the two girls unpacked their gear and focused on the GWB.

The suspension bridge was basically four huge cables strung from shore to shore over two giant towers. The massive structure had two separate decks with many lanes of traffic flowing in both directions.

"What exactly is it that we're looking for?" asked Robbi as she played the lens of her telescope across the bridge from end to end. "You don't expect that guy with the calluses to be hanging around here all day, do you? Not that he could even if he wanted to. I mean, look at all that traffic."

The morning rush hour was in full swing and the inbound cars on the upper deck were parked bumper to bumper. The lower deck didn't look much better, but at least it was creeping along.

"I told you, I'm not really sure what we're looking for," said Cleo, "but I need to check the place out. I thought it over last night and there's no possible way that I can be around to stop anybody, but maybe I can figure out how to get pictures of the dognappers and their van. That way the police would have a chance of catching them." She looked over at her friend. "What do you think about the idea?"

Robbi was nodding her head while keeping one eye glued to the telescope. "Okay, so what is it that I'm looking for?"

Suddenly it was clear in Cleo's mind. "I need to find someplace with a clear view of that upper deck, close enough to see the cars and the people as they make the swap." She looked through her binoculars. "I sort of hoped I could do it from here, but even with a serious zoom lens, I wouldn't get enough detail in the pictures. It's just too far to the bridge and there's too much stuff in the way."

"Stuff? You mean like cars and cables and those humongous towers?" asked Robbi. She put down her telescope and started laughing. "It's gonna be pretty hard to get a picture without any of that 'stuff' unless you go up on the bridge and shoot down."

Robbi was joking, but as Cleo looked at the cars inching along the bridge, she realized that her friend had hit the nail right on the head. The only unobstructed location was from above. Somehow she had to get up onto the bridge itself.

Cleo panned her binoculars up the nearest tall tower, searching for a ladder or a walkway, when she saw the answer. High up on a platform, laid across one pair of cables, a maintenance crew dressed in orange coveralls was painting the bridge. They looked like tiny ants crawling on a vast web, but when Cleo focused her binoculars, she could make out a row of rungs along the tower that served as ladders for the men.

She tilted her binoculars down to the Hudson River far below. It was incredible to think the work gang must be over three hundred feet above the surface of the water. She couldn't even imagine being that high up, but the more she scanned the bridge from end to end, the more she realized it was the only place to get what she needed. She and Robbi watched the men work for over an hour, until they knew precisely what Undercover Cleo's next move would be.

Cleo thought her friend was going to collapse from excitement. Robbi hadn't stopped talking long enough to even grab a breath since the girls had decided on a plan for that evening, and the teen detective was certain that by this time her friend's brain was oxygen-deprived.

"So," said the exuberant girl, "where should we go first? Eighth Street or Madison Men's Shop?" She didn't even give Cleo a chance to answer. "Eighth Street. You know how long it always takes us there."

Knowing Robbi had already made up her mind and that there would be no changing it, Cleo agreed and the girls took the subway all the way down to the Washington Square stop, four blocks from their destination. The Village was one of their favorite areas, and they headed directly for a small shop that had great prices.

Eighth Street was a circus of shoe stores and the merchandise seemed to change daily. After Robbi purchased a pair of pole climber work boots, which she assured Cleo she had been intending to buy for quite some time, the two girls proceeded to check out the rest of the shops for the very latest in trendy and mostly affordable shoe styles. Tucked between the shoe stores were other shops that sold a potpourri of goods from T-shirts to jewelry to posters. The friends made sure they didn't pass up a single one of the closet-sized stores or any of the stands on the street, which was where Robbi found a rather frightening silver earcuff—a spider with dark red jeweled eyes.

"I've got to have this," she declared. "What do you think?"

Cleo thought it was pretty creepy, but it definitely fit her friend's style. "Nice," she said, looking at a small silver butterfly charm. Cleo knew it was corny, but she felt that it symbolized her own changes. Her undercover adventures had somehow given her a new confidence. Even her mother had recently mentioned that Cleo's posture seemed to be getting better.

At less than three dollars, the charm was a real bargain, so the teen bought the tiny medallion, less than half an inch in diameter, and fastened it onto one of the safety pins she kept on the belt loops of her jeans.

She decided it would be her own secret memento, a private reminder of her alter ego, Undercover Cleo.

By the time the girls were sure they'd seen every item for sale along Eighth Street, it was well past lunchtime. They stopped in a Bagel Buffet for a couple of inexpensive hot dogs that they could munch on their way to 14th Street. There, they caught a bus that took them west to their next destination.

Madison Men's Shop was a funky little store on the West Side Highway that specialized in workman's clothes. Cleo and Robbi had come here once with Carver, Robbi's older brother, when he was looking for a genuine Carhardt jacket. The coats were really warm and sturdy and Cleo had to admit, they also looked pretty sharp on him. The girls had had fun exploring the shop that was jam-packed with every kind of workman's gear, including hard hats like the men on the bridge had worn.

The proprietor, a white-haired gentleman who looked as if he'd missed his last few hair appointments, climbed a rickety ladder to pull down a stack of hard hats in a variety of colors. The girls chose two along with pairs of orange coveralls and were relieved to find the prices fit their budgets. After Cleo's makeup purchases and "Amira's" wild cab ride, she didn't have much allowance left, and Robbi had just spent most of hers getting the boots.

Time was definitely running short and the girls hurried back to the Upper West Side. When they reached the Richards' brownstone on 86th Street, it was just about the time they would normally be returning from school. They scurried into the house and started up the stairs.

"Well, well, well," came a voice on the verge of laughter, "it looks to me like you two children didn't exactly come home from good old Walton now, did you?" The two friends were shocked to see Carver standing on the second-floor landing.

Cleo looked down at her hands holding the bag with the hard hats, and over at Robbi who carried the large bag with her boots. There was no disguising the fact they'd been out shopping.

"What are you doing here?" demanded Robbi. She'd gotten over her fright and had shifted to her pick-a-fight mood. She always got riled up when her brother, who was only four years older, called her a child.

"I think I asked you that first," said Carver, sitting at the head of the stairs. He looked extremely amused, but Cleo could see he wasn't about to let Robbi get out of this too easily.

"Well," started Robbi, "we did go to school. We just happened to, uh, find some stuff at a really neat store on the way home. You know, along Broadway."

"Uh-huh," said Carver. "I thought you walked home on West End Avenue." He beckoned for the girls to come closer. "Let's see what you've got."

"No!" said Robbi a little too quickly. "I mean, it's not really any of your business." She clenched her hand around the top of the brown bag from the downtown shoe store and pulled back.

Carver jumped up and chased the girls who screamed and bolted down the stairs and into the basement family room. The boy ran the two friends around the pool table a few times, then Robbi made a mad dash for safety.

"Follow me, Cleo!" she yelled as she headed back up the stairs toward her fourth-floor bedroom. The problem was, Robbi could only go so fast with her short legs, and Cleo could see that she was doomed.

She followed her friend, but Carver was right behind her in seconds. "Come on," he said. "I just want to know what is so important you two had to cut classes to go buy it." He dove for Cleo's bag, ripping it and sending the two hard hats bumping down the spiral staircase.

All three kids stared as the hats rolled down to the floor and came to a gently rocking stop.

"Hard hats? You bought hard hats? What are you guys planning to do? I happen to know those aren't exactly the latest fashion in headgear, not that that would ever stop a wacko like you," he said, looking at his sister. "So why don't you tell me what this is about." He looked dead serious now.

In fact, Carver looked like he'd wait all night until he was satisfied with an answer. Sometimes he acted more like a parent than an older brother, which was totally annoying.

The teen detective's mind was racing to come up with a plausible excuse when Robbi opened her mouth. "Look, Carver," she said, "we need them for something we're planning this evening and if we don't hurry, we won't make it. Yeah, we cut some classes, but it's for a good cause, to help a friend and that's all I can say, except that obviously we bought the hard hats so we can do this safely, okay?" Amazingly, she had managed to say everything without pausing for a breath, as if it was one long, exceptionally speedy sentence.

Oh, great, thought Cleo. She couldn't believe her friend, the Queen of Wild Imagination Land, had actually chosen this moment to tell the truth.

"That sounds pretty lame," said Carver. "Anyway, Dad has hard hats. You know that."

"Not the right color," said Robbi in a small voice, "and don't ask any more questions or I'll tell Mom and Dad about you-know-what . . ." She cut off her sentence and stared defiantly at her brother.

Carver sucked in his breath. "Okay, okay," he said, putting up his hands in surrender. "Look, then, can I do anything to help you? I mean, if you tell me what you're planning, maybe we can figure out something safer."

"No, thanks," said Cleo at the same time that Robbi said, "Actually, yes." She had perked up when she realized her brother was going to let her get away with this. "I didn't think you were going to be home so I was just gonna take them, but Cleo needs to borrow one of your blue workshirts." The Richards family all had outfits for working on the house.

Carver nodded. "Go ahead, there's one in my dresser. Listen, I gotta say, I don't like this a bit, but I've got a huge term paper due next month so I'll be here working on it. If you need anything, I mean anything, you call me, okay? Dad's not going to be home until later tonight, he's got a dinner at the firm, so you're clear until about 9:30, 10:00." Mrs. Richards was still starring in the Broadway play, *Murder in Park Hill*, so she was never home until around eleven. The two girls nodded, then scampered off to get ready.

"Is he really gonna let us go without asking any

more questions?" said Cleo as she donned the painter's outfit.

"Of course," said Robbi. "Don't you think I've covered for him, too? I know you think my brother's perfect, but let's get real. He owes me, and big time."

She didn't offer any further explanations and Cleo was once again left to envy the relationship between Robbi and Carver. For all their brother/sister bickering, the two made no secret of the fact they adored each other.

At 4:30, the two girls went out the front door of the Richards residence carrying their backpacks containing photo gear and their hard hats. When they reached the George Washington Bridge, the girls were glad to see the workers had already left for the day, but the platform remained in place. It was surprisingly easy for them to make their way to the maintenance entrance of the bridge at 178th Street and walk into the empty employee work area.

"You know what," said Robbi, "I'm suddenly not so sure about climbing up there. I feel an attack of acrophobia coming on even as we speak."

"Stop it," said Cleo. Though she'd always worked alone in disguise, this plan required a pair of workers. One of the things the girls had noticed earlier that morning was that the bridge employees only worked in groups of two or more, which meant that going solo would be sure to draw attention. Cleo knew she was taking a risk by asking her friend to join her, but she also felt it would be safer for two of them to be up there. That way one could concentrate on snapping photos of the ransom exchange while the other could focus on safety.

They walked to a check-in gate that was labeled DANGER—BRIDGE EMPLOYEES ONLY.

"Get me out of here," said Robbi under her breath but she kept walking toward the entrance.

A group of five men and one woman came out through the door, obviously on their way home for the day. Several of them had IDs clipped to their pockets. They were engrossed in conversation but one of the men glanced their way.

"Doing a night shift?" he asked.

"Yeah," said Cleo, making her voice as low and gruff as she could manage.

The girls had carefully splattered silver-gray paint on their orange coveralls and hard hats and even on their shoes. Cleo was wearing her old Timberlands and had expressed concern about the newness of Robbi's pole climbers, but her friend had joyously "custom-colorized" the boots. The friends knew they blended in with the other employees, but as they neared the person manning the checkpoint, Cleo realized it wasn't good enough.

"Quick, put your subway pass ID in your hand," she whispered to Robbi. Trying to look businesslike, the girls took their IDs out of their jeans pockets.

Cleo watched another group coming out. "Slow down," she rasped. "Follow me and do just what I do." As this group passed by, Cleo moved to the far side of the entrance gate, keeping the people coming out between herself and the person manning the checkpoint window. Cleo flashed her ID up over her head. "Night shift," she said.

Robbi aped her friend, holding her ID as high as she could. Her voice cracked as she called out, "Night shift," but the man never even bothered to look up. They were through.

Cleo followed a series of signs that read TO BRIDGE—UPPER DECK.

A brisk wind, strong with the smell of the river, hit them the second they came out of a door onto a metal catwalk that was nothing more than an open grating. Hundreds of feet below them were the gray rippling waters of the Hudson. As they had seen the workers do, the girls fastened around themselves their safety harnesses, taken off the rack on the wall, and clicked them onto a safety cable that ran along the narrow walkway.

"This is kind of like gym class, you know, when you're walking on the balance beam?" said Robbi. "Only here it's for keeps." She looked at her friend. "I've just developed a strong dislike for gymnastics."

Before her friend had a chance to back out, Cleo nudged her on toward a set of rungs at the base of the tower. When they reached them, they stopped and looked up. The top of the ladder actually disappeared into the low-hanging haze. "Maybe I should wait down here?" suggested Robbi in a very tentative tone.

"Then we both get caught," said Cleo. "Go on, you first." She unhooked her safety harness from the walkway line and reattached it to a safety line that followed along up the ladder.

The climb to the scaffolding was both dizzying and terrifying. More than once the girls had to stop to catch their breath and reassure one another they were doing the right thing. But as each rung brought them nearer to the top, Cleo began to realize that the journey was one of the most exhilarating things she'd ever done, and she could tell that Robbi felt the same way. It wasn't hard to understand how the bridge maintenance crew could continue to come out here day after day to work in the sky.

Finally they pulled themselves onto a wide platform suspended by small wire cables. The girls realized that they were actually hanging from the massive twin steel cables that supported the weight of the north side of the bridge. Their platform swayed gently in the breeze, but as they'd hoped, they had a perfectly unobstructed view of the entire upper deck. No matter where the two cars stopped, Cleo would be able to photograph the exchange.

The girls refastened their harnesses to safety lines that circled the platform, and sat down to unpack their backpacks. Cleo took out her father's camera and his 500-millimeter zoom lens, then pulled out her binoculars while Robbi took out a large but empty paint can. As the teen detective peered through her binoculars, Robbi knelt and pretended to paint. There was nothing for them to do now but wait.

Forty-five minutes later Cleo felt her heart jump. Approaching the bridge from the east, from the direction of Manhattan, was the gray van.

Chapter 20

Cleo swished-panned her binoculars toward 178th Street, but there was no sign of the gold Rolls. *Oh, no,* she thought. *What if Mr. Edsel-Mellon doesn't show.* She glanced at her watch and realized it was still early.

"Now keep yourself calm," Cleo said out loud for her own benefit as much as for her friend. This was just the kind of situation where Robbi got overly excited and Cleo didn't want a disaster at three hundred feet up. "Look over there." She pointed in the direction of the van, then carefully returned the binoculars to her bag.

Robbi took out her telescope and aimed it where Cleo had been pointing. "That's it, right?" she asked.

"Right."

Cleo could feel her breath coming in quick short gasps and willed herself into a calm state as she picked up the camera and trained it down onto the bridge below. She checked the exposure, like her dad had taught her, and focused on the vehicle as it pulled into a lane cordoned off with orange cones so that repairs could be made on the road. Without the camera the cars looked like toys but the long lens brought them in until they filled her viewfinder. Cleo snapped a photo, then her attention was caught by a flash of light.

Changing the focus of the zoom lens, she saw the light was the sun reflecting off the chrome trim and windshield of a black Rolls-Royce limo. *Of course,* she thought. She'd been expecting the gold Rolls, but hadn't Lilliana said that the glitzy car was for her and JP? This had to be Mr. Edsel-Mellon.

A moment later she watched the sleek limo pull in behind the battered van. A burly chauffeur stepped out of the driver's seat and opened the door for Mr. Edsel-Mellon.

Lilliana's father carried a large brown paper sack that looked heavy. He walked to the front of his car and waited for someone to come to him. It didn't take long for a man to get out, then grab a pet crate from the rear of the van before approaching Mr. Edsel-Mellon.

Cleo clicked away.

The man from the van wore dark glasses and a large-brimmed hat so it was nearly impossible for Cleo to get a clear shot of his face, but she knew any pictures might be helpful to the police. The man opened the carrying case, then Mr. Edsel-Mellon leaned over to look inside. He straightened up and nodded his head. Next he held the paper sack open for the dognapping suspect to check.

Both men appeared satisfied and the exchange was made simultaneously, hand to hand. Everything seemed to go perfectly and in moments both cars were speeding off. Cleo breathed a sigh of relief and put down the camera.

"Hey, you two!" It was a man's voice and it was coming from below.

The girls froze, then Cleo ventured a peek through the grating of the platform. "Yeah?" she answered.

A man halfway down the ladder was making notes on a clipboard and looking up at them. "Your shift was over an hour ago," he yelled. "Go on home."

Cleo smiled and gave him a thumbs-up. "On our way." She hoped the man wouldn't wait for them and was grateful to see him scurry down the ladder like a kid on a jungle gym.

The girls made their way back as fast as they dared. It was getting dark quickly and the area around the bridge wasn't the safest part of town for two young girls. They jogged back to the subway station and were more than happy when they finally got on a southbound train.

The doors opened at the 86th Street stop and Robbi stood to get off when Cleo grabbed her friend's arm. "Come over for dinner," she said. After what they'd been through this evening, it would be really nice not to have to eat solo.

Robbi felt exactly the same way. "Yeah," she said. "That'd be totally great. But remind me to call Carver, otherwise he'll be sitting around and worrying."

Cleo agreed and the girls rode on to 72nd Street. They were both ravenous after their catwalk climb and were discussing what Nortrud might have made for dinner when Cleo unlocked the door to the Olivers' apartment. There was an unusual aroma in the air and to Cleo's surprise she heard her parents talking in the kitchen.

"That you, Cleo?" called her mother.

The girls looked at each other, then down at their coveralls, knowing there was no way to change before they went in to say hello. At least they weren't wearing a makeup disguise as well. A dozen excuses flicked through Cleo's mind as she and Robbi walked to the kitchen.

"Hi," she said.

"Hi, Mrs. Oliver. Hi, Mr. Oliver," said Robbi.

"Robbi," said Cleo's mom, giving her a hug. "Nice to see you. Are you staying for dinner?" The girls often ate at each other's homes, and both sets of parents were glad to have an extra body at the table.

Robbi and Cleo both nodded.

"So, what's with the goofy outfits?" asked Mr. Oliver. He was chopping salad vegetables furiously while Cleo's mother sat at the kitchen table in front of a very thick novel. "Oh, no, no, don't tell me," he continued, doing a whiny impression of Cleo, " 'Dad, this is what *everyone's* wearing to school now.' "

Cleo was embarrassed to hear her father's silly and annoying imitation. "Da-ad," she said. "I was just helping Robbi paint her room." It was the perfect excuse, especially when coupled with one of Cleo's favorite techniques for not answering questions. She'd found if she changed the subject and asked her own question, her parents often forgot who was under interrogation. "Dad, are you cooking dinner tonight?" She eyed the bottles of herbs, spices, and condiments her father had lined up on the counter. This didn't look good.

"Chef Oliver at your service," answered her father in a bad French accent. He was really in a weird mood tonight.

"You might want to go home for dinner," Cleo whispered to her friend. She didn't mean to be rude, but Scott Oliver had a way of concocting truly inedible meals.

"I beg to differ," said Cleo's dad in a pompous tone, as a piece of tomato went whizzing off his cutting board and stuck to the kitchen wall. "I assure you that this will be a fine repast, one fit for a king."

Mrs. Oliver leaned in to her daughter and Robbi. "Nortrud did mention that there was some rosemary chicken," she whispered. "It's in the fridge . . . just in case."

Cleo had forgotten about yesterday's dinner, and was relieved to have a viable option for her dad's creative cookery. She snatched two carrots, handed one to Robbi, then sat next to her mom.

"So," said Mr. Oliver, "any news from your little friend on the dognapping story?"

Cleo nudged Robbi and gave her an eye message to keep quiet, then she took a bite of carrot and munched slowly before answering. The teenager had to be sure not to give her father any reason to suspect what they had been up to. "Uh, yeah," she said. "They were supposed to get Bilbo back yesterday at some party, but I don't think it happened. Lilliana called and said something went wrong. I think maybe they were gonna try again." She gave Robbi another look that warned her not to say a syllable more than that.

"Well, if this is anything like most kidnappings," said Mr. Oliver, "they don't have much time left. I'd venture to say that dog is going to be stew before long."

"Scott, please," said Cleo's mom, looking up from her novel.

Robbi giggled, but Cleo was horrified by her father's attempt at humor. "Dad, that's gross," said Cleo. The remark would have really bothered her if she hadn't witnessed the exchange of Bilbo and the ransom money earlier in the evening. *Which reminds me, Lilliana must be really happy right now,* thought Cleo.

The phone jangled at that moment and the girl leapt up to answer it. "Hello?"

"Hi, Cleo, it's me," said Lilliana. To Cleo's surprise, the little girl sounded like she was crying.

"Hi, can you hold on for a second?" Cleo had a feeling this was a call she'd better take in private. She gestured for Robbi to follow, then carried the phone into her bedroom. After kicking the door shut, Cleo sat on her bed. "Hi, Lilliana, what's wrong?"

"You'll never believe this," the girl answered through a series of sniffles. "Everything's a total goof-up now. Daddy met the man on the bridge tonight and gave him the money, except it was only some of the money. He said he'd put some real stuff on top, and the rest was fake bills. He also said he checked to make sure it wasn't a toy dog again before he paid, but, Cleo . . . it isn't Bilbo."

"What do you mean?" asked Cleo.

"It looks just like him, but it's a girl dog. Now, I don't know if I'll ever get Bilbo back."

Cleo did her best to comfort the little girl, but there really wasn't much she could say. There was, however, something she could do. She had the film with pictures of the two suspects, their van, and its license plate. The photo stores were closed by now, but Cleo made a mental note to drop off the film first thing in the morning.

"Don't let me get to school tomorrow without taking this in," she told Robbi, holding up the roll she'd removed from the camera.

"Put it in the shoes you're gonna wear," suggested Robbi. "That way you can't forget it."

"Good idea," said Cleo. She set the film in the heel of her sneaker, then sat back as Robbi dialed home.

Of all nights for her parents to be home. Cleo usually loved the evenings when her mom and dad were at dinner because between the articles her dad researched, and the madness and eccentric personalities of her mom's world of high fashion, the conversation was pretty terrific. Unfortunately, tonight Cleo didn't have time to sit and listen to idle chatter, and with Robbi as an added dinner guest . . .

The girl put her head in the palms of her hands. It was going to be a long night.

Ten minutes later Alexa called the girls to dinner. Mr. Oliver had fixed some sort of casserole and though it actually looked normal, Cleo had learned not to overestimate the dishes her dad devised.

She served herself a judicious portion, but before venturing a taste, she poked through the noodles in an attempt to identify as many of the ingredients as possible. Cleo could clearly see chopped carrots, onions, peas, mushrooms, and ground beef, in a tomato-based sauce. So far, so good. Then she noticed the familiar dark, juicy-looking tidbits and thought, *Oh, no, he didn't.*

But he had. Raisins lurked everywhere, hiding in the mess. Cleo's dad had an irrational urge to put raisins in practically every dish he dreamed up and while Cleo didn't actually dislike the little dried fruits, there was a time and a place for everything. She snuck a peek at Robbi who was taking an extra large helping.

I'm dead, thought Cleo. Could there be anything more embarrassing than having a best friend over for dinner, then serving her an utterly bizarre meal? Cleo closed her eyes as she saw Robbi lift her fork to her mouth.

"Wow, Mr. Oliver," said Robbi, "this is great."

The weird thing was, Cleo knew that her friend really meant it. *Leave it to Robbi,* she thought. *Probably the only human being on earth besides Dad who would enjoy this mishmash.* One at a time Cleo pushed the raisins off to one side of her plate and nibbled on a noodle, wishing she could have some of Nortrud's rosemary chicken.

Even though Cleo still had strategizing to do on the case, she soon found herself not wanting the dinner conversation to end. The talk had turned into a lively discussion of musical styles through the years with Mr. Oliver demonstrating his own version of doo-wop, rock and roll, disco, even rap. Cleo had been mortified at first, but relaxed when she realized Robbi was really enjoying the live performance. In fact, at one point, everyone got into it and Mr. Oliver's song became a quartet with the whole table warbling at the top of their lungs.

It was goofy but enormously fun, and Cleo couldn't remember when she had laughed so hard or so long. It was a real letdown, even though her stomach muscles were aching, when Mrs. Oliver finally mentioned the time.

Mr. Oliver took Robbi down to the lobby and put her in a cab, but not before Cleo gestured to her friend that they should talk later. After waiting a reasonable amount of time for Robbi to arrive home, Cleo took the portable phone into her room and dialed.

Robbi picked up before the first ring had finished. "Today was awesome, wasn't it?"

"Yeah," Cleo agreed, "it was, and I hate to ruin it, but we've got to talk about tomorrow."

"Tomorrow?" echoed Robbi. "I am not skipping classes two days in a row. I mean, today was definitely great, but no way am I getting expelled."

Every so often, Robbi surprised Cleo by being logical and even a little stuffy. The odd thing was, Cleo was also surprising herself these days by being amazingly gutsy.

"You don't have to cut any classes," said Cleo. "I just need to run a couple of ideas past you." Throughout dinner her father's words about Bilbo having limited time had kept flashing in her head. "We've got to find the people who have Bilbo."

"I thought that's why we went to the GWB today," said Robbi. "Shouldn't those pictures do the trick?"

"Maybe," said Cleo, "as long as somebody cares as much about that puppy as we do. I mean, we can make sure Detective Milton gets the photographs, but I have the feeling Bilbo isn't very high on NYPD's priority list."

"Well, you're definitely right there," agreed Robbi. "Finding a dog couldn't be anywhere as important as catching murderers and stuff like that."

"It is to Lilliana," said Cleo. "Anyway, I have an idea of where to start looking for our pair of suspects. Where would you go if you wanted to get a look-alike dog, quickly and cheaply?"

"How should I know?" asked Robbi. "The ASPCA or someplace like that, I guess."

"Exactly," said Cleo. "Tomorrow we start making phone calls."

Robbi agreed to take half the list so the girls could do a lot of calling on breaks between classes. "But what are you gonna do if we find the place?" she asked Cleo.

"I don't know," Cleo admitted. "Any suggestions?"

Of course Robbi had plenty of really wild ideas, but nothing that Cleo thought would work. The two friends finally hung up with the teen detective still uncertain about her next plan of action.

Cleo climbed into bed and pulled her journal from its hiding place. She was still keyed up after the events of the day, and knew it was a perfect time to write in her book.

The journal had been a gift from her mother on her thirteenth birthday and was one of Cleo's most treasured possessions. Mrs. Oliver had included a note that said she knew her daughter was entering a very special but sometimes difficult period in her life.

"You might not want to write every day," her mom had written, "but there will be experiences you'll want to remember. It's also a good place to put down your dreams, wish lists, or secrets. Believe me, I know there will be times when there is so much going on in your head that you can barely deal with it, and it often helps to be able to sort it out on paper."

Cleo had had diaries, of course, when she was younger, but it had seemed like a chore to write in them and she had always given up after a month or so. This time, she'd made a decision to write only if she felt the need, and it soon became a habit. Sometimes the act of writing felt as good or even better than talking to a close friend.

Cleo ended her entry for the day, then tucked the blue journal back in its narrow drawer. She had to get some sleep, but still hadn't the slightest idea what she would do, even if she found out where the fake Bilbo had come from. She'd probably just have to call the police.

A short while later, a huge smile played across Cleo's face. Was it the answer? She lay awake for a few more minutes contemplating her latest plan until she reached for the lamp. In moments, she had fallen fast asleep.

Chapter 21

It was Cleo who struck gold the next morning. Her call to the ASPCA on East 92nd Street yielded the information that a small white female dog fitting Bilbo's description had been adopted only the day before.

"I've got to go," she told Robbi after hanging up the phone. "Will you put this in my locker?" She handed her backpack to her friend who grumbled good-naturedly but disappeared with it up the stairwell.

Earlier Cleo had packed a large handbag full of clothes and she hurried off with it toward the first-floor rest room. Class was just about to start so she would only have to wait a few seconds before she had the place to herself, but in those few seconds she overheard something that rocked her world.

"I'm telling you, JP said he's in love. Supposedly he met this Indian girl at some party."

Cleo couldn't help jerking her head sharply in the direction of Chandra Fisher and her best friend Hayley Alexander, two of Walton's cheerleaders. Even though the day had barely begun, the girls stood at the mirrors reapplying their lip gloss. They didn't take the slightest notice of Cleo, who couldn't decide whether being ignored was a good thing or a bad thing.

Everyone's love life was subject to public scrutiny at Walton, so Cleo didn't try to hide the fact that she was eavesdropping as Chandra described how she'd overheard JP tell another student he had a huge crush on some girl named Amira.

Cleo told herself this was only thirdhand gossip and probably not true. She knew how whisperings could get stretched and bent completely out of shape, but as the cheerleaders giggled their way out of the room, Cleo couldn't help but feel a little flattered at the idea that someone just might have fallen in love with her.

The door swung shut, reminding her she was alone, and she quickly donned several thick sweaters and a gray skirt borrowed from her mother's closet. Thick support hose and a pair of Nortrud's sensible crepe-soled shoes completed the picture of a woman who dressed for function and comfort rather than style.

Cleo was startled to see in the mirror that she now had a thick torso and skinny limbs, a look not uncommon for a woman of middle age. She took off the hat she'd worn to school, revealing subtle gray streaks she'd combed in that morning with shoe polish. Now it was time to create a middle-aged face.

She used several shades of foundation to give herself an uneven skin tone, then drew in age lines around her mouth and eyes. A touch of blue eye shadow went on next, then she powdered over everything to give herself a papery look of older skin.

She noticed the powder had all but erased her thick lashes, a plus in this case, and she decided not to add any mascara. A splash of fuchsia lipstick, some heavy-framed glasses, and her work was done. Undercover Cleo threw the handbag over her arm and peeked out the rest-room door. When she was sure the coast was clear, she scooted rapidly out a side door and flagged down a taxi along West End Avenue.

In the waiting room of the ASPCA, a heavyset woman sat at a small desk in a room filled with cages of dogs and cats up for adoption. The woman peered at Cleo through silver cat-eye glasses that had tiny rhinestones at the outer corners, and Cleo could see that the lady had taken great pains with her hairdo. The receptionist's gently permed silver curls were held in place with a beaded hairnet—an accessory that could only be purchased in the most old-fashioned of drugstores. She looked up and smiled warmly when she saw Undercover Cleo enter. "Yes? May I help you?"

"Hello, I'm Detective Martin," the teen said as she briefly flashed a badge she'd plucked out of one of her father's desk drawers. Sometimes her father's pack rat habits came in pretty handy. The girl took out a pen and notepad and expertly flipped it open. "I'd like to ask a few questions about an adoption that I understand took place yesterday." Undercover Cleo spoke in a gravelly voice colored by a Queens upbringing.

"Oh, yes," answered the lady whose name tag read MARJABELLE LEWIS. "They just told me someone from the 21st Precinct might be dropping by." The receptionist stood and smiled at the "detective." "You certainly got here fast, I'll say that." Several bangles on the woman's wrist clinked together as she gestured for Undercover Cleo to sit in the chair facing her desk.

21st Precinct? A major panic surge jolted Cleo's body. She'd never specified which precinct she was from, nor had she said anything about stopping by when she'd called the ASPCA from school this morning. It had to mean that someone from the 21st was on their way over. Undercover Cleo suddenly realized she'd better get what she needed and get out fast.

"I think I'll stand," "Detective Martin" said. "I really can't stay long, I just need some answers to a few quick questions. Now, what exactly can you recall about the individual who adopted this particular dog?"

"Well, the lady was very specific about what she wanted, even brought in a photograph, one of those Polaroids," said Marjabelle.

"Do you have a description?" asked Undercover Cleo.

" 'Bout my height, five-two, but real tough-looking," said the woman. "Even wore overalls, the type that kids wear nowadays except hers had some nasty green stains on the knees. She wasn't dressed at all appropriately for a woman of our age. I'm sure you know what I mean." Marjabelle gave "Detective Martin" a knowing look.

The girl stifled a laugh. "I do. But now, what else can you tell me about this woman?"

"She had black hair, I'd say *bottle* black," Marjabelle specified as her hand unconsciously went to her own well-teased coif. "She had a nice tan, but if you ask me, I'd say she was spending a bit too much time in the sun. Leathery skin and hands with lots of scrapes and calluses. Oh, and she wore a real ugly watch."

"Watch?" "Detective Martin" placed her palms on the desk and leaned down. "What kind of watch?"

"Big," said Marjabelle. "Looked like a man's watch. Dirty leather band. I myself think jewelry should be a little more feminine. I suppose that's why I noticed." The woman glanced at her bangle-filled wrist and smiled.

Undercover Cleo forced herself to remain calm. "Would you happen to have her name and address on file?"

Marjabelle nodded. "I thought you'd be wanting that." She reached to pull open her drawer.

"Excuse me?" said a high male voice that was frighteningly familiar.

Undercover Cleo turned slowly to see Todd Milton coming in the doorway. The girl gulped and hoped her voice would work. She needed to get out the door and fast.

"Why don't you go ahead and help this gentleman while I make a phone call?" said the "detective." "I did see a pay phone out in the hall, didn't I?"

Marjabelle nodded and turned her attention to Detective Milton. "And what can I do for you, sir?"

Cleo walked as fast as she dared around the gigantic man. When she was sure she was out of sight, she bolted for the door.

A young couple was just getting out of a cab in front of the animal shelter, and as soon as they were clear, Cleo jumped in. "Upper West Side," she said to the driver, "and move it."

As the taxi pulled out onto 92nd Street, the girl heard a high-pitched shout. Detective Milton lumbered out of the building, waving his arms at the departing cab, but there was no way he was going to catch Cleo now.

She pulled her makeup removal kit—tissues and cold cream—out of her bag and worked quickly to erase the years she'd added to her face this morning. Then she slipped off everything but her bottom-most sweater, changed her shoes, and yanked her baseball cap back down over her streaky hair. She checked her hand mirror. Yes, she'd pass muster at Walton, although there was a definite sparkle in her eyes and a color in her cheeks that she usually didn't have.

She had the cabdriver drop her off at Central Park West and 86th, just in case Detective Milton had gotten the cab number from the couple who got out. It hadn't taken nearly as long as she'd thought and after walking the rest of the way to school, she found she'd missed only three classes, one of which was study hall. Unfortunately, she was just in time for history.

It was hard to concentrate on the droning voice of her teacher, especially when Cleo kept thinking about what she had learned at the animal shelter. She was annoyed at having to leave without getting the watch woman's name and address, but she reasoned that the information would probably be false, anyway. There was no way the dognapper would have given the ASPCA her real name or address.

It looked like the woman wearing the old watch had been present at three different events connected to the dognapping. A nice lead, but where did it get her?

Cleo knew there was something more in all the bits of information she had, she could feel it. She just couldn't put it together. The teen detective spent the rest of the day at Walton running the pieces of the puzzle over and over in her mind, but when the final bell rang, she was nowhere near a solution.

On the way home, she picked up the photos from the film store. She flipped through the pictures and saw that because of the extreme distance, her snapshots were very grainy. There was a shot that showed the license plate of the truck, but it had been obliterated with mud or something else. Still, the photos would probably serve their purpose. The stocky man's face was at times obstructed by the hat, but there were two good face shots and the driver of the truck, though half in shadow, could be identified as a woman. Cleo thought it might be possible to identify both suspects from the photos.

She kept one complete set of the pictures and sealed a duplicate set into a plain white envelope. She was anxious to get home and call Lilliana to check on the status of Bilbo, but she had to get these photos to the police station ASAP. The problem was, she didn't want to go anywhere near the stationhouse. She'd already had one encounter today with Detective Milton.

No, it would definitely be tempting fate to make an appearance at the 21st Precinct house.

Cleo took a deep breath and made a decision to risk the extra day by mailing the photos. She addressed the envelope to Detective Milton, then bought a stamp in a stationery shop on the way home and dropped the photos in a corner mailbox.

As she arrived home, Cleo was distracted from making her phone call to Lilliana by a ruckus coming from the TV room. "Dad's playing video games again, isn't he?" she said to Nortrud who was industriously cleaning a smoky antique mirror hung in the foyer.

The housekeeper nodded with a pained expression on her face. "I don't know what's worse, when your father has got too much work or too little."

Mr. Oliver was more obsessed with video games than anyone Cleo knew, with the possible exception of Michael Payton, a boy at Walton who was among other things a computer and video game whiz kid. If her dad was between writing projects, it was a good bet he could be found in front of the television or his computer engrossed in some game.

The girl walked into the TV room to find her father wrestling with the game controller as if his life depended on it, grunting and yelling when the characters didn't react as he'd intended. It always made Cleo and her mother laugh when Mr. Oliver insisted that his playing was a form of relaxation, especially considering that he'd broken a half-dozen controllers in various fits of temper.

Her dad looked up as Cleo entered the room, then he pushed the pause button on the controller. "I'm stuck on this level," he complained. "What am I supposed to do?"

He was deep into his latest role-playing game and, as usual, had a chair pulled up directly in front of the television set. Cleo slid her pack off onto the sofa and sat on the floor by her dad's chair.

"Okay," she said, "did you cut down all the grass over there?" She pointed to a section of the screen, then watched as her father manipulated the little knight character to swing his sword so that all the grass and flowers in the area disappeared in a series of sound-enhanced *whooshes*.

"I don't see anything," said her dad, who could rarely count patience among his virtues.

"Just keep going," said Cleo. She didn't like to give her dad hints that were too specific. To Cleo it seemed like cheating.

"My character's going to have blisters on his little hands if he doesn't find something soon," complained Mr. Oliver. "He's probably already got a crop of calluses."

Cleo rolled her eyes and watched as her dad neared the hidden door to the fourth kingdom, when it hit her. *That's it*, she thought. *It's the calluses.* Both the stocky man and the woman with the watch had callused, battered hands and harsh weathered tans, exactly like her Grandfather Oliver who owned a huge farm in Nebraska. They also had a van. Maybe the dognappers were gardeners.

Chapter 22

The more she thought about it, the more it all seemed to fit. The overalls with their green, perhaps grass stains, even the beat-up van that would be ideal for carrying lawn mowers and leaf blowers. And what about the Green Machine? Who better than a gardener to infiltrate the organization? Suddenly Cleo found herself wondering if the mysterious Green Machine member, "Jeannette Collins," had also sported a leather-strapped watch.

One question Cleo still had was: why? Why would a gardener commit a dognapping . . . unless they had been employees of the Edsel-Mellons. Maybe the boat stewards weren't the only ones unhappy about their wages.

"Aha!" yelled Mr. Oliver. The exclamation was accompanied by a vigorous stomp of his foot. "I've got it!"

Phoebe, who had been napping along the TV room wall, responded immediately. The vibrations of the stomp were a match for a rabbit-foot warning thump and the bunny leapt up wide awake. One floppy ear shot up, wired into a full upright position and the other ear pitched straight forward.

Cleo couldn't help bursting out in a fit of laughter. "It's okay, Feeb," she said. She walked over to her pet and gathered up the furry beast in her arms.

The girl could see that her father was well into the game again, squinting and puffing as if he were personally wielding a sword and fighting evil magicians. With Phoebe in her arms Cleo tiptoed out of the room. Right now the teen detective needed to speak to an expert on the lives of the famous, including the Edsel-Mellons. She went to find Nortrud.

The housekeeper was lying on her stomach in the living room vacuuming under the sofa. It was an altogether undignified position for a woman of the housekeeper's beefy build, and Cleo had to bite her tongue not to laugh.

"Nortrud," said the girl, "do you happen to know if the Edsel-Mellons have any gardens?"

It took the woman a full three minutes to return to a standing position. "Gardens?" she said, rubbing her back. "Now where on earth did that question come from?"

Cleo put on her most blankly innocent expression and shrugged. "I don't know," she answered. "I was sort of wondering if Lilliana had to walk her dog on the street like everyone else in New York, or if she had a backyard." She hoped she appeared casual, because she was thinking, *Every move I make in this house is under a magnifying glass.* Between her reporter father and mother hen Nortrud, Cleo had to disguise even her most offhand comments, while Robbi could blurt out practically anything at home, and still get away with it.

Luckily, Nortrud didn't press Cleo any further. "Well, now, I believe the family lives over on the East River and if I recall rightly, it's some sort of brick house with a small garden of sorts. Well, you know, it's as much of a garden as any place has in the city."

So they must use gardeners to maintain the area, thought Cleo triumphantly.

"But if you want to talk gardens, the family just bought a big estate on Long Island last fall. Supposed to have fabulous landscaped grounds."

"Uh-huh?" Cleo didn't see how a gardener who'd only worked for the Edsel-Mellons for a few months would be a likely suspect, but it never hurt to have more information.

"The family hasn't moved into the house yet. There's some serious redecorating going on, I think," said Nortrud. "In fact, I've read that this particular estate has been empty, unoccupied I should say, for years. Caught up in some sort of litigation, but it's been maintained perfectly. I read there's a hedge maze and it's even rumored that there's a secret garden somewhere on the property."

Cleo nodded, hoping the housekeeper would remember more. This was getting interesting. "A secret garden?"

"No one's ever seen it, supposed to be a secret that comes with the house. Don't know if it's true or not."

"That is so cool," said Cleo. She wanted to hear more but at that moment the phone rang.

The girl ran to the kitchen and picked up the receiver. "Hello?"

It was Lilliana. "Hi," said the girl. "Sorry to keep bugging you."

"No, it's okay," Cleo assured her friend. "I was going to phone you." She felt bad that she'd been so caught up in her father's game that she'd forgotten to call. "Any news?"

"The dognapper lady just phoned and said they knew Daddy was going to give them the fake money, and that's why they brought the fake dog. She promised they'd outsmart Daddy every time and said we only have one more chance. They're gonna call again after the weekend."

Cleo couldn't figure out why the dognappers wanted to wait through the weekend. *What is that all about?* she wondered, but there wasn't time to dwell on the question. It wasn't yet five o'clock, and the teen detective knew it was still possible to catch people before they left work.

Her first call was to the Green Machine to follow up on one of her hunches. The phone was picked up after only one ring. "Hello, Green Machine. Denise speaking."

"Hi, Denise," said Cleo, speaking with the somewhat older but enthusiastic tones of her young reporter character. "This is Josie Silverman. From *The New York Daily Press*? I met you last week."

"Oh, sure, Ms. Silverman," answered Denise. "What can I do for you?"

"I just wanted to ask you a few follow-up questions," said "Josie." "Has Jeannette Collins turned up, by any chance?"

"Well, no, actually she hasn't," Denise admitted. "But that's not all that unusual. I don't mean that our members disappear regularly, but we often get volunteers who don't have a lot of money, or are in between jobs. They help us out when they can."

Cleo doubted this was the case with "Jeannette," but she kept that thought to herself. "I understand, Denise, but let me ask you one more thing. Did this Jeannette wear any distinctive jewelry?"

"Well," said Denise, "I don't know if you'd call it jewelry exactly, but she did wear a big watch. Big white face and an old leather strap. Looked like maybe a man's watch. I thought maybe it was her father's or something sentimental, but I never asked her about it. She was kind of a private person, kept her distance."

Cleo thanked the girl at the Green Machine headquarters, then hung up slowly. Pieces were starting to fall into place, but "Josie" still had one more call to make.

Pulling the cream and gold invitation from her desk drawer, Undercover Cleo dialed the number for the

Edsel-Mellon mansion and asked to speak with the secretary, Elaine.

"Speaking," said the secretary. "Who is this and what is it concerning?"

"Josie" introduced herself and explained that she was doing an article on the finest gardens in and around New York. "I'm just getting started," said the "reporter," "and it would be a real coup for me if I could tour the Edsel-Mellons' homes."

"Too late," said Elaine. "If only you'd called last week. We've already been contacted by *Estate* magazine, and they're sending one of their new writers over on Saturday to meet our press agent."

One thing Cleo had learned during her undercover adventures was to be flexible. If she couldn't go as "Josie," maybe she could go as this other reporter. She decided to smoke out the name of the person from *Estate* magazine. "Oh," she said, "well, thanks anyway. I guess they're sending my friend Tammy. Looks like she beat me to the punch again."

"Tammy?" said Elaine. "No, I believe the writer's name is Jim. Jim Smith."

Chapter 23

"A guy?" asked Robbi with a laugh as the two girls hurried from homeroom to math class. "Nice. Guess you can't use Undercover Cleo this time. What are you going to do?"

"Well, I really think my theory about the gardeners is a good one," said Cleo. "I've just got to figure out a way to find them."

Just as the girls turned a corner someone rammed into them sending Robbi to the floor. "Hey," she cried out, "watch where you're going." Robbi stood up quickly, rubbing her wrists. "You're lucky I'm okay."

JP Edsel-Mellon was also in a heap on the floor sitting in a pile of schoolbooks. "Sorry," he apologized. "You sure you're both all right?"

Cleo, the only one who'd managed to stay upright, stared at the boy. This did not sound like the JP she'd tried to talk to last week. He would never have apologized, much less asked how anyone was doing. "We're fine," she answered. "You?"

"Yep," said the boy. He smiled, then looked quizzically at Cleo. "It's Cleo, isn't it? You know, you remind me of someone. My girlfriend, actually. I mean, you sort of remind me of her. She's a lot older though."

Cleo was in total shock. "You have a girlfriend?" she asked.

"Yeah, she's really cool. Her name's Amira and she's from India."

Cleo gasped and stepped on Robbi's foot to keep her quiet. How could Amira be JP's girlfriend when they'd only barely met? It was tempting to pop the boy's delusion, but there was no way to do it without revealing Undercover Cleo. Besides, the teen detective found herself feeling massively flattered.

"Uh, that's nice," said Cleo. "By the way, how's your sister?"

"Not bad, but she won't stop talking about that dog. My dad's doing everything he can to get her to forget about it. He and Natalie are taking us to Disney World this weekend, which they hope will take Lilli's mind off Bilbo. I don't think it'll work though. Sometimes it's hard to forget someone you love."

This time, the two girls couldn't hide their amusement and their big smiles shook JP out of his daydreaming. "I'd better get to class," he said. The boy picked up his books and continued down the hall.

"Well, that was bizarre," said Robbi, looking after JP.

"That's for sure," said Cleo. It was hard to believe

this was the same snooty boy she'd spoken with last week. Something he had said disturbed her though. "Robbi, if Mr. Edsel-Mellon is trying to get Lilliana to forget about Bilbo, it seems to me that they've given up on the dog." If this was true, Cleo had to redouble her efforts to find Bilbo.

Saturday morning, Cleo was up before the crack of dawn. She was about to begin one of her most challenging makeovers and hadn't slept much at all from nerves. She put on several layers of undershirts, then dressed quickly in jeans, shirt and tie, and a suede baseball-style jacket. Then she pulled her hair back in a low ponytail, being sure to use a plain rubber band she'd taken off of the stack of mail.

Now it was time for makeup. After applying a thick, slightly darker foundation, Cleo used a natural sponge to stipple on a very faint five o'clock shadow. She shaded the sides of her nose so it appeared long and thin, then used darker foundation to flatten out her unusually high cheekbones. Next, she took a small paper bag, a purchase she'd made the day before, out of her backpack and stared at the contents.

"This had better work, Cleo Oliver," she told herself. She was having serious doubts about pulling this one off and hadn't even brought Robbi into the plan. She wasn't sure her friend would be very supportive this time.

Gingerly Cleo unscrewed the top of a little bottle and applied spirit gum, a clear tacky adhesive, to her upper lip. Then she picked up the small mat of hair she'd bought and stuck it on her skin.

The fake mustache didn't look half bad the way it was, but Cleo took her manicure scissors and trimmed it, appllying more makeup to blend in the edges. It felt like she had a caterpillar on her upper lip. She'd been clever in buying a mustache that was not a perfect match for her own black tresses. In her reading on disguises and quick changes, she'd come across the strange fact that a man rarely has the same color hair on his head as on his face because different genes controlled the color and texture of hair for different areas of the body.

Cleo applied smaller wisps of hair to her eyebrows, extending them in slightly. She didn't want to give herself a "monobrow," but she did want a more masculine look. She debated wearing a baseball cap and glasses, since both were great ways to hide facial features, but decided they might only call more attention to the fact she was in disguise. She decided that in this case she would not hide behind any props.

She peeked out of her bedroom door, and after listening to make sure that her parents were still asleep, she snuck out of the apartment.

"Jim Smith's" cab pulled up in front of the Edsel-Mellon home at 8:30, just in time to see Pepper, the press agent, emerge from another taxi. The man turned around and smiled as Undercover Cleo stepped onto the sidewalk.

"You must be Jim," said Pepper. "Pepper Charvet." He extended his hand and shook briefly. "Come on in."

Cleo was ecstatic to have passed her first test. The

press agent had simply assumed she was a man. "Quite a pleasure, I'm sure," she said, using her deepest voice and a light British accent. She knew that would make her seem more sophisticated and might even impress Pepper. Then she added yet one more layer to her disguise: "Jim" limped up the stairs.

"Thanks for seeing me so early," "he" said.

"Quite all right," said Pepper. "We're just so pleased that *Estate* wants to do a spread on the new digs." He took out a set of keys and let them in, which was a great relief to Undercover Cleo. She had been worried about getting past the ID-checking butler, Mr. Filbert. Cleo had doctored her father's press card but it might not have passed a close inspection. This was perfect.

Yesterday Cleo had called the real Jim Smith at the offices of *Estate* magazine and pretending to be Elaine, the Edsel-Mellon's secretary, she'd postponed Jim's meeting with Pepper by a week. After that, posing as Jim Smith's assistant, she'd called Elaine to arrange to meet Pepper at an earlier time. Cleo needed to make sure she wouldn't run into her parents as she rushed out of the apartment wearing, among other things, a mustache.

As it turned out, Pepper fell all over himself trying to impress the writer. He talked nonstop about the Edsel-Mellons and their impressive homes, not to mention himself and how hard he worked to maintain the public's image of the wealthy family.

Undercover Cleo was treated to an extensive tour of the East River home. She enjoyed getting detailed explanations of the history of each work of art and who had designed the fireplace, who had cast a particular piece of stained glass and so on.

"Here's something you and your readers might enjoy," said Pepper when they reached Mr. Edsel-Mellon's office. The man walked over and pushed a button on one of the bronze sconces and to "Jim's" surprise, a section of the oak panel wall slid open.

"A secret passageway?" asked the "writer."

"Exactly," said Pepper. "We suspect it was put in so the original owner could spy on his guests. It leads to the office next door which at one time was the receiving room. Just one of the fun details of the house." He smiled, obviously enjoying the opportunity to reveal the sliding door to "Jim."

The press agent continued the tour of the house and was so busy talking that he never did look closely at "Mr. Smith." An hour later the tour was concluded and Pepper and "Jim" set a date for the "writer" to return with a photographer in tow.

"The secretary mentioned I might visit the Southampton estate this afternoon, yes?" asked "Jim."

"Of course," said Pepper. "I'm sorry I won't be able to go with you today, but I'll have the decorator notified that you're coming for a prelim look-around."

"Fab," said "Jim." "Just one more thing and I'll be on my way. I've heard ever so much about the magnificent grounds of the Long Island home, would it be possible for me to interview the Edsel-Mellon gardeners?"

There was a slight pause before Pepper answered. "The Edsel-Mellons don't employ any gardeners."

Chapter 24

"You're not telling me the Edsel-Mellons do the gardening themselves, are you?" asked "Jim."

The PR man laughed. "Well, as a matter of fact, Mrs. Edsel-Mellon does tinker in the 'garden' here, though why anyone of her stature would want to get dirt under her fingernails is beyond me." Pepper glanced down at his own manicured hands. "Would you like to see for yourself?"

He led "Jim" toward the backyard without waiting for an answer. "As for the Southampton estate, well, it was purchased in late fall when there was really no need for groundskeepers so they were laid off for the winter. Just recently, Mrs. Edsel-Mellon decided that she preferred to hire her own staff for the place, so everyone who had worked for the previous owners—

housekeepers, groundskeepers, handymen—were all let go. She's started interviewing just this week, I believe."

Undercover Cleo was silent for a moment. So the Edsel-Mellons had fired a whole staff. The teen detective realized that she'd just been handed a fresh group of suspects. It was too much to fathom at the moment and the girl decided that for now she'd concentrate on her gardener theory.

"I see," said "Jim." "Well, in writing my article, it would be quite helpful to at least speak with the former gardeners since they'll be the ones who will be the most familiar with the grounds. Would it be possible to get a list of names and addresses?"

"I'm sure it would," said Pepper. "Elaine's the one who'd have that information. A-ha, here we are."

They had reached the tiny backyard and it was immediately clear why no gardener was needed. There were two large trees that shaded the entire area, leaving only enough room for four tiny flower beds. Most of the area was covered with a mosaic of multicolored slate slabs, which actually looked quite nice since moss had filled in the cracks between the stones.

"Charming," said "Jim." "I'm quite sure our readers will enjoy seeing the contrast between this and the magnificent grounds in Southampton. Which reminds me, I really need to get going if I'm to make it out to the Island, but I really do want to get in touch with those gardeners. You said Elaine would have the information, but is she in today?"

"Oh, yes," said Pepper. "No rest for the weary. Between Mr. Edsel-Mellon's development project and the new estate, we've been buried by work. Then of course there's all this hullabaloo over that wretched dog." He shivered. "Can't say I'm disappointed not to have the mutt running around underfoot. I never expected my job description would include walking the family dog."

"Jim" forced a sympathetic smile. She was wondering if Pepper hated the animal enough to be a part of the dognapping. "You had to walk Bilbo?"

"Oh, yes," said Pepper. "Whenever Carl wasn't around to watch after Lilliana, she'd come around and ask me to go with her. Dogs *and* children. Ugh. She snuck that beast along with her everywhere. Everyone on the staff knew it, but I was the one who had to deal with it, one way or another."

Undercover Cleo thought quickly. Pepper had definitely not been in the van either after the midtown party or at the bridge, but that didn't necessarily mean that he wasn't involved. She suddenly found herself wondering if this squeamish and pristine man could have masterminded the whole thing.

"Elaine," said Pepper after he'd led the "writer" back to the offices, "this is Jim Smith, from *Estate*." He waited while the two had exchanged the customary pleasantries. "He needs to speak with the former gardeners out in Southampton."

"Jim" smiled. "I'm sure you understand. I really need every little detail about the history of the grounds. My readers expect that."

The teen detective thought there was a momentary lapse in the secretary's composure, but in the blink of an eye Elaine was shaking her head slowly. "Oh, I am sorry, but I wouldn't have the slightest idea where to find them. I believe most of the employees lived at the estate, but they were all given notice and had to move out."

Undercover Cleo was disappointed, but at least she had a starting point. She knew that the best way to locate a missing person was to start with the last known address and now that she had directions to the Edsel-Mellon estate, she was set.

"Jim Smith" thanked both Pepper and Elaine for their time, then as quickly as possible, considering his limp, the *Estate* magazine journalist went down the stairs and out the front door.

Instead of going home, Cleo went directly to the Richards' brownstone. Having removed her facial hair and makeup in the bus on the way over (something she was getting to be quite adept at), the teen detective hopped lightly up the stairs to the front door and rang the bell.

"Cleo," said Mr. Richards when the door finally opened. "You're bright and early this morning. Come on in, I think Robbi's still having breakfast."

Cleo went straight to the kitchen where Robbi and Carver were seated at opposite ends of the table reading sections of the Sunday *Times*. Cleo had always thought it was crazy that most of the New York Sunday paper arrived on Saturday, but her father had explained to her that there were two good reasons. One was that so many elements were needed for the Sunday edition that the deadlines had to be spread out over several days, and the other was that it was much easier to deliver the bulky newspaper over two days instead of one.

"Hey," said Carver, barely glancing up.

Robbi was in the middle of a bite of sausage and merely looked up and waved.

"Hi," said Cleo, taking a seat.

"You know, I hate to break this to you, Cleo," said Carver, "but that outfit isn't the most flattering thing in the world. You look like a guy. Ow!"

Robbi had tossed an orange and hit her brother in the head. "That is like so rude, Carver," she said. "He didn't mean it, Cleo. I think it's a great look."

To everyone's surprise, Cleo burst out laughing.

"See what you did," said Robbi to her brother. "Your comment drove her off the deep end." She looked worriedly at her friend. "You okay?"

Cleo wiped the tears from her eyes. "Yeah. I'll explain later," she said and eyed her friend's plate. "Aren't you done eating yet?"

Robbi sighed. She had been contemplating an extra helping of rice and another two sausages, but she could tell that Cleo needed to talk. "I guess so."

The girls stood to leave the kitchen, but not before Robbi had given her brother a sisterly whack on the arm. He responded with a missed swat at her leg, and the girls scooted up the stairs.

"So, what's the scoop?" asked Robbi after they'd retreated into her bedroom.

Cleo shocked her friend when she revealed her most recent disguise. "So it was actually good that

Carver said that about this outfit," she said. "I mean, this morning I was *trying* to look like a guy."

"Sometimes you frighten me," said Robbi solemnly.

"So," said Cleo, "the thing is, don't you think that we should get out to the estate?"

"Definitely," said Robbi. "Are you going as Jim Smith, though? I mean, isn't that who they're expecting?"

"Yeah, that's who they're expecting," said Cleo, "but I think it's too risky to try and fool a lot of people with that disguise. I think we'd better just get out there and poke around."

"Okay," said Robbi. "But, Miss Superhero, I think there's just like one major problem you haven't thought about: How are we supposed to get out there? Flap our arms and fly?"

"Well," said Cleo, "that's kind of what I need to talk to you about. Since it's a private estate, we really need to get there by car. My parents are taking one of their day trips to Pennsylvania to hit the tag sales, so our car is out. Do you think we could maybe, like, borrow your parents' car?"

Robbi narrowed her eyes and stared at her friend. "Yeah, I'm sure they'll let us borrow it, but do you really want Carver to drive us all the way to Southampton? I don't know if he'll go for that without having to know every detail. You'd have to let the cat out of the bag, as they say."

Cleo pretended shock. "Carver? Why would we need him to drive when I can do it myself?"

Chapter 25

"You're not serious," said Robbi, aiming a doubting stare at her friend.

"Yeah," said Cleo, "I am. Don't you remember my dad taught me to drive last summer? Wants me to be ready since you can get your license when you're fourteen in Nebraska." She rolled her eyes even though she'd loved the lessons. "Plus you know I've been driving Gramps's tractor for a long time now."

Robbi crossed her arms over her chest. "Well, the driving age might be fourteen in some places, but might I remind you, that here in New York state it's sixteen. Even then you can't drive late at night or in the city until you're seventeen."

Cleo put on her most sincere face. "Well, we'll be there before it gets too late and we won't really be driving in the city. We'll actually just be trying to get out of it." She knew she was using Robbi's own brand of twisted logic, but Cleo hoped it would work to convince her friend that this was the only way they'd get to the next step in solving the mystery.

The teen detective could see Robbi still had misgivings about pulling this stunt off, but finally she acquiesced. After making sure that Carver was nowhere around and checking to see that both her parents were sufficiently occupied, the tiny teenager snuck the car keys off a hook in the kitchen closet.

"As long as we're in the kitchen," she said, remembering the second helping she'd passed up at breakfast, "we might as well pack a lunch."

Just in case, the girls made a couple of sandwiches apiece, and grabbed some oranges, four cans of soda, and a package of cookies. They knew it was going to be a long drive, and the fewer stops they made, the fewer their chances of getting caught.

First they took the bus down to Cleo's so she could change her clothes. The teen was still wearing several things she'd borrowed from her father's closet, and when she heard her parents talking in the kitchen, she quickly slipped into her bedroom to change. Emerging a few minutes later, definitely feeling more "Cleo," she and Robbi went to see her mom and dad.

"Aren't you the early bird this morning?" said Alexa as the two girls came in. Cleo's mom and dad were just cleaning up from their morning meal.

"Yeah, well, guess I don't need my beauty sleep as much as you two old fogeys," said Cleo. It wasn't her usual brand of humor, but she was feeling extra confident from her morning's success.

"That's certainly true," said Alexa with a laugh. "Listen, us 'old fogeys' were thinking of taking the weekend off. We thought we'd stay up in Pennsylvania for the night, come back tomorrow afternoon. Want to join us?"

When Mr. Oliver had the time and Mrs. Oliver was in town, they often took spur-of-the-moment weekend trips. They loved driving to Upstate New York or into Pennsylvania with no particular destination in mind, and they'd invariably return with a car packed with "treasures" that they'd found at flea markets and garage sales. Cleo hated to pass up one of these weekend trips with her parents, but today there was no choice.

"Thanks, but Rob and I have plans," said Cleo, "and actually, would it be okay if she spent the night?" This could turn out to be just what she needed.

"Absolutely," said Mrs. Oliver. "In fact, I'll feel better knowing the two of you are here together."

Cleo grinned at her friend, then gave both of her parents a hug. "We'll be fine," she said. "Have a good time, and I'll see you tomorrow."

Minutes later Cleo and Robbi were out the front door of Cleo's apartment building and on their way to pick up the Richards family car. Unlike Cleo's dad, Robbi's family kept their car in a garage on West 57th Street.

Parking in Manhattan was exorbitantly expensive and Scott Oliver refused to pay the high prices that garages charged, especially for a dented and dinged-up eleven-year-old vehicle. As a result, he parked on the street, which meant that he had to move the family car every few days to accommodate the city's alternate-side-of-the-street parking rules that were made to allow street cleaning. Some days, Mr. Oliver spent as much as forty-five minutes driving around looking for a space to put his car.

Cleo's dad had an alarm on the old Hyundai and as an extra added precaution against it being stolen, he also pulled a certain fuse so the car wouldn't start. Cleo couldn't imagine why anyone would ever bother to steal the beat-up clank mobile, but her father had assured her it was worth several thousand dollars in parts alone.

"You'd better take these," said Robbi as they rode the garage elevator up to the fourth level, and with a frown she handed her friend her parents' car keys.

Cleo unlocked the door and climbed into the driver's seat. She realized it had been much easier posing as Jim Smith than it was to sit here behind the wheel of this two-ton metal monster. Driving the backroads of Nebraska was one thing, but driving the streets of New York City was definitely not for the faint of heart. The teenager inserted the key, closed her eyes, and turned.

The roar of the car startled her and she was glad this wasn't the type of garage where an attendant brought the car around. It would have been much more nerve-wracking to test out her driving skills, or lack thereof, in front of some garage employee.

Cleo stepped on the brake, put the car in reverse, and felt it jerk. She slowly lifted her brake foot and let the car inch backward. The girl stepped on the brake and even though she'd only given it a light tap, the girls were thrown forward against their seat belts.

"Whoa there, boy," said Robbi. "First-degree whiplash and we're not even out of the parking space. I thought you said you knew how to drive."

"I do," insisted Cleo, "but it's been a while and I'm a little nervous."

A horn beeped and she turned to see another car coming down the aisle. She bit her lip, then shifted back into drive and the car scooted forward into the parking space.

When the car was gone, Cleo resumed her efforts and after much maneuvering was able to get the car out of the space and facing in the direction of the exit arrows. It took fifteen minutes, but she was getting used to the brake and actually managed to drive up to the attendant's window fairly smoothly. As they approached, Robbi reached into the glove compartment.

"Here," she said, "hand this to the guy." It was a parking card.

The young man took the card from Cleo, swiped it through his machine, then handed it back to the girl. When she tried to take it from him, he didn't let go.

"You're not the usual driver of this car, are you?" he asked.

Cleo's throat was suddenly so dry she couldn't speak. Luckily, Robbi didn't have the same problem.

"Hey, come on," she said, leaning over Cleo. "You

remember me, right? This is my brother's girlfriend, Cleo."

"Oh, right," said the man. The story seemed to satisfy him and he waved the girls on.

Cleo's face was flaming red from being introduced as Carver's girlfriend, but she did her best to maintain her composure as she pulled out of the garage. She drove east along 57th Street and was glad not to be in heavy weekday traffic.

"You're doing pretty good," commented Robbi.

Cleo turned to smile. "Thanks," she said, just before a tiny sports car cut in front of her and pulled to a quick stop.

She jammed her foot on the brake so hard that she thought her leg would go through the floorboard. The station wagon screeched and slid to a stop only inches from the sports car's bumper. Cleo dropped her head onto the wheel, then looked over to make sure her friend was okay.

"I'd say you could apply for a license to drive a taxi and pass with no problem," said Robbi. She attempted to laugh, but Cleo could see she was shaken.

"I don't think you'd better distract me anymore," said Cleo. "I almost reduced that Miata to roadkill." Her knuckles were white from clutching the wheel.

After that, Cleo seemed to do much better. She kept her distance and by the time the girls had passed the Queensborough Bridge, the teen detective was driving like a pro, at least a New York City–style pro. No one paid the slightest attention to her veering or her last-minute lane switching and she was even confident enough to listen to Robbi chattering along the way.

Cleo found that the expressway driving was the easiest of all, but she still had to concentrate just to keep the car in the middle of her lane and drive exactly at the speed limit.

Robbi surprised herself and Cleo by doing a commendable job as navigator and three hours later they reached Southampton. Robbi managed to read both maps and Pepper's directions that led the girls to a beachfront, along rows of ocean-front mansions.

"This is amazing," said Robbi. "Stop for a sec, okay?"

Cleo pulled the car to the side of the road where they could look out on an endless row of mansions with the blue-green sea in the background. Together, the girls sat and stared, a little awed by the magnificent vista. Most of the estates were painted white and in the crisp afternoon sun their walls dazzled in the brilliant light.

"If you squint your eyes and move your head real fast, side to side, it looks like a bunch of big teeth," said Robbi. Cleo's friend had a way of coming up with observations that were really weird.

"Yeah, if you say so," Cleo told her friend, though she herself couldn't see a resemblance to anyone's mouth. She started up the car again and the girls continued down the road.

As they drove, they noticed the houses were spaced farther and farther apart until finally the girls pulled up in front of a huge open iron gate between two monolithic stone posts. There was no house visible from the road.

"This is it," exclaimed Robbi, pointing to weathered brass numbers on one of the posts. "I did it!" She was overjoyed at having directed Cleo to the right location. "You may thank me now."

Cleo rolled her eyes and laughed. "I suppose I did nothing here," she said.

"Well, all you had to do was steer in the direction I told you," stated Robbi. "I'm definitely the real hero." She obviously wasn't a person with the problem of low self-esteem.

"Whatever," agreed Cleo. The teen detective stopped directly in front of the gates. She was sure they'd been left open to admit the decorator and, of course, Jim Smith, but certainly not two teenaged girls. It was tempting to drive on in, to at least get a preliminary look at the estate, but Cleo decided they had better find a different way in. She shifted into reverse and backed up.

"Hel-lo?" called Robbi. "Didn't I just say this was the place?"

"Yeah," said Cleo, "but we've got to get in some way so that no one sees us. There are workers here today, remember? Don't put away that map, Indiana. Before we go waltzing in, we've also got to find someplace to hide the car."

Robbi grumbled but unfolded the map once again. "Well," she said, "there's definitely a beach behind the house somewhere. Keep driving around the side. There should be a small road leading to the water."

Sure enough, it was little more than a dirt path but it led the girls in the direction of the ocean. Soon after they turned off the main road, the girls parked under some trees and trudged over the sand toward the water. The sea breeze came at them with a clear, clean smell of salt and sun.

"It looks like we're in luck," said Cleo. It was a long flat beach that ran for miles in both directions, uninterrupted by any sort of fencing. "We'll definitely be able to get onto the Edsel-Mellon estate from here."

There was no response so she turned around to see Robbi tiptoeing close to the water's edge, peering into the sand.

"What are you doing?" called Cleo.

Robbi looked up and ran over to her friend. "Just looking for beach glass. I was thinking, if I could get enough that were sort of the same size, I could use them as buttons for that jacket I just bought at the Salvation Army."

It sounded like kind of a neat idea, and as they walked toward their destination Cleo helped her friend comb the beach for the little chunks of polished glass. They'd found two when the teen detective glanced toward the land. Perched upon the highest point around on a rise of rock and sand, its large windows staring out upon the endless expanse of the Atlantic Ocean, was a whitewashed brick mansion the size of an airplane hangar.

Chapter 26

"Wow," said the girls with a single voice. The Edsel-Mellon house looked like something out of an old-time storybook.

Robbi pocketed her button collection and the girls marched up the sandbanks toward the landscaped grounds that separated the beach from the house. They soon found themselves strolling in a perfectly kept English garden.

The plants were caught up in the early surge of spring. Bordering pebbled walks were raised flower beds of every imaginable geometric shape. Some were filled with daffodils and tulips, while others were bare and seemed hungry for the care of a groundskeeper.

There were also high hedges that separated the huge estate into many smaller gardens. "We could wander this place for centuries," declared Robbi.

Cleo didn't doubt it. She glanced up at the house that was clearly visible from every point on the grounds, and saw they could always make their way directly to it if necessary. While they still had daylight left though, the teen thought it wouldn't be a bad idea to investigate the gardens. Besides, the house might still be full of workmen.

Cleo and Robbi wandered back and forth, marveling at the intricate layout of walks and foliage. They strolled the walks between herb gardens and flower beds until they suddenly found themselves standing at an arched entrance that led into a catacomb of tall and dense prickly bushes.

"The hedge maze," said Cleo, remembering her conversation with Nortrud.

"Too cool," said Robbi. "Just like in the movies."

It was more than cool, but Cleo wondered if they'd be able to find their way out once they entered. It would be horrible to have come all this way, only to get stuck in a labyrinth of thorn-covered foliage.

"This looks endless," said Cleo. "Talk about getting lost forever." On the other hand, it would still be a few hours before they could get into the main house unnoticed, and to Cleo the idea of trying to solve the maze was unbearably tempting. She eyed Robbi, who wore her most pleading look.

"Please, pretty please, please?" begged Robbi. "Maybe we'll find some sort of clues in here."

"Yeah, right," said Cleo. It was beyond doubtful they'd find anything in the overgrown maze, but she couldn't deny the fact that in the back of her mind, she was thinking about the secret garden. What better place to hide it than in the middle of this endless maze?

She looked up before entering and noticed that the large trees planted here and there among the ten-foot-high hedges effectively blocked any aerial view of the maze. "Let's walk around it first, okay?"

The girls walked the edge of the hedges to get an idea of its actual size. It took them over half an hour just to circle the perimeter and they counted two separate entrances on each of the five sides. They peeked inside each entrance and saw nothing but untrimmed walls of brier with prickles that would go right through anything but the heaviest clothing.

When they had just about made their way completely around to the farthest point from the house, they poked their heads in the tenth entrance. To their surprise, they saw fresh clippings on the ground. Someone had recently been trimming the spring twigs.

The girls looked at each other in amazement. "This is the entrance we go for," said Cleo. "We can always follow the trail of clippings back out."

Robbi nodded. "Like Hansel and Gretel and the crumbs."

Arm in arm, they went under the brier archway. The trail of clippings took a crazy route, twisting and turning and leading them deeper and deeper into the maze. The girls pressed on and were soon completely disoriented. After walking for forty-five minutes, all the while following the serpentine path of clippings, it suddenly came to an end. Cleo and Robbi stopped and stood still, surrounded by hedges on three sides and facing a dead end.

"Give me a break," said Robbi. "Someone trimmed this path for nothing? What kind of a dorkhead would do that?"

Cleo shook her head. It didn't make sense, but they were definitely facing a blank hedge. "Well, at least we can find our way back out," she said.

Robbi threw a mock tantrum. "No, no, no," she cried. "I wanted to get through to the other side." She banged her fists in the air, then kicked at the dead-end hedge wall.

There was a solid thunk, though her foot should have been connecting with soft foliage. "Ow!" she yelled. "What kind of bush is that?" She rubbed her toe and glared at the offending plant.

"That didn't sound like any bush to me," said Cleo. She walked over to the green wall of briers and carefully put her hand in between the wiry branches.

There was something solid behind the greenery. Cleo pried the vines apart and saw weathered wooden slats behind the hedge. "No way," she whispered. "Rob, I think there's some kind of gate here."

Robbi immediately poked her own hands into the hedge. "Omigosh," she said, feeling the boards, "this could be amazing. Unless, of course, there's a wooden wall that runs through the middle of all the hedges." She pushed a foot into a section of hedge off to one side and her shoe easily went through until her calf was stuck with a half-dozen thorns. "Ouch!"

Cleo was now feeling around where she thought a door handle might be. "Eureka!" she cried.

She moved apart the vines to show Robbi a tiny white porcelain doorknob with a faint pink rose in the center. Cleo wrapped her hand around the knob and turned.

She'd expected it to be locked. That's the way it worked in that book anyway, but to her surprise the knob turned. With a peek back to Robbi for a dose of encouragement, she pushed. The hedge here was attached to the door and everything opened at once as she stepped forward.

Cleo and Robbi entered a small area, about fifteen feet square. A white iron bench sat in one corner under a miniature rose tree, and Cleo recognized gardenia and star jasmine bushes, but much of the area was still unplanted. In the middle of the garden was a tiny white marble statue of a girl on tiptoe holding a wand. She looked as if she was blessing the space all around her. The girls walked up to inspect the beautiful centerpiece, then gasped. Right behind the statue was a small doggie dish.

Cleo knelt beside the dish that had two sections to it. A thin film of water was in one of the bowls and there were a few nuggets of dog food in the other. "Rob," she said, "I think someone was keeping Bilbo here." Her case against the gardeners had reached a new plateau.

The girls checked the rest of the area carefully but found no other clues. Reluctantly, after taking a last look around at the special place, Cleo and Robbi left, being sure to close the hidden door tightly behind them.

By the time they followed the clipping path out of the maze the sun was casting an orange light across the grounds. As the girls started toward the main house, they could feel a keen wind coming off the water and they zipped their jackets and put up their collars.

After walking up a set of steps to a terraced area just behind the house, they looked back on the gardens they'd just come through.

"That's some backyard," said Cleo. She grabbed Robbi's shoulder and pointed. "Hey, look, that must be the cottage."

"Now we're sure no one's home, right?" asked Robbi. Her courage always seemed to wane as the sun went down.

"Pretty sure," said Cleo teasingly. "No, seriously, I don't see any lights going on. It's probably okay."

They were rapidly losing daylight, and the girls took off across a gravel path toward the servants' quarters that were built of the same white brick as the main house. On the way, Cleo couldn't help fantasizing about how great it would be if her parents owned an estate with a separate little house just for her.

The girls found the front door of the little cottage was slightly ajar and cautiously they pushed it open and stepped inside.

"Flashlight time," announced Robbi. There was still a dusky glow outside, but indoors was a different matter.

The girl pulled her light from her backpack and played it around the room. Cleo did the same thing and they soon realized the place had been recently vacated. Sheets had been thrown over the furniture, but there was no sign of cobwebs or even much dust. Cleo picked up a corner of one of the sheets and saw an intricately carved Victorian love seat. She was admiring the piece when Robbi reminded her that they were there to look for clues.

"Oh, yeah," Cleo said. She ran her hands around the seat cushions, but came up empty.

The two girls methodically lifted sheets and checked drawers, cupboards, and spaces behind cushions, but it wasn't till they got upstairs that they found anything useful.

There was a pile of junk mail in a small wastepaper basket under the desk, a tiny butler's table. The girls whooped with joy as they picked out the envelopes addressed to Alice and Archie Cobb.

Chapter 27

"What do you want to bet that Archie is short and thick, and Alice wears a big watch with a leather strap?" asked Cleo as she flipped through the mail.

"We just may have IDed our dognappers," agreed Robbi.

"So what else do you think this will yield?" asked Cleo, reaching into the garbage can again.

"Ugh," grunted Robbi, "I don't know, just don't ask me to stick my hand down there."

Robbi was being overly dramatic as usual. Cleo didn't really see anything wrong with poking around in a simple office wastepaper basket. She might have felt differently if it were a kitchen trash can, but even then, if it would help her find Bilbo, well, she might not like it, but she'd do it.

The only thing left in the garbage can was a

wadded-up piece of newspaper. Cleo carefully unfolded it and spread it out over the floor.

"Classifieds?" she said. She checked the date and saw it was from the previous week's Sunday *Times*. "Alice and Archie were here last week. We can't be that far away."

She smoothed the paper and scanned it rapidly. On the opposite side, nine ink circles on the page caught her eye.

"Look," she said, pointing them out to Robbi, "these are help wanted ads and get this, some of them are for gardeners to help with weekend 'spring cleaning.' No wonder they couldn't arrange another exchange until after Monday."

"They're working part-time," said Robbi in a ponderous tone. "So, do we assume that they got at least one of these jobs they were looking for?"

"Well," said Cleo, holding up the newspaper, "we do have a list of phone numbers here. It'd be easy enough to check, wouldn't it?" She high-fived her friend. "We might even be able to find the Cobbs tomorrow, if they work Sundays. What do you say we make a few phone calls?"

She went to the phone in the bedroom but found it was dead.

"What about the main house?" suggested Robbi. "I mean, if they're doing work and all, they'd need to have a working phone." It made sense and after they neatened up the gardeners' cottage and left it exactly as they'd found it, the girls headed toward the mansion.

By now, the sun was almost set and the girls took a moment to watch the flaming orange ball drop out of sight over a magnificent purple and red sky to the west. Then, starting to shiver, they raced each other to the main house.

"Do you think we can get in?" asked Robbi. The girls were standing outside, looking through the French doors that led into the ballroom.

"As long as we can find an open window or door," said Cleo. "Pepper said that the Edsel-Mellons are having a new security system put in this coming week, so I think right now we're safe."

The girls walked the outside of the house until they spotted a window on the second floor that had been left open. Cleo looked around for a way up, when Robbi tugged on her sleeve.

"Look," she said, aiming her flashlight up. A trellis that would soon be full of blooming wisteria climbed from the first floor to almost the third. "Think that'll hold us?"

Cleo shone her light along the fragile ladder. It didn't look all that sturdy. She walked over and pulled on a low rung that creaked under the strain.

"I don't think so," she said regretfully.

"Well, what about me?" said Robbi. "I bet I could get up, especially if I go fast."

"Are you sure you want to try?" asked Cleo. She played her flashlight beam in Robbi's direction and saw her friend's face was a mask of determination.

Robbi handed Cleo her pack, then started up. The trellis crackled and popped but as Cleo kept her flashlight trained ahead of Robbi's path, the girl scrambled upward and soon disappeared into a window.

"I'm in," Robbi called in a loud stage whisper. Suddenly it didn't seem right to talk in full voice.

Cleo waited for about five minutes, then jumped when she heard a noise behind her. It was Robbi opening a large set of doors to a ballroom.

"Enter my humble abode," said the small girl.

The girls took a leisurely, self-guided tour of the forty-room mansion. They counted seventeen fireplaces, including one in a huge master bathroom equipped with a modern Jacuzzi.

"I think we'd better make our phone calls and then get out of here," said Cleo when she was satisfied that she'd seen every room.

The ballroom appeared to be the center of operations for the construction work and it was there that the girls found a telephone. The first call yielded an answering machine. The girls exchanged a worried look, hoping they wouldn't get nine answering machines.

A woman answered the second call. Cleo pretended to be a friend of Alice Cobb's. "I'm driving them to the job tomorrow and just want to make sure I have the directions," said the teen detective.

"I don't know what kind of joke this is," said the woman. "I hired someone else for the job."

"Strike one," said Cleo to Robbi, who crossed one entry off the list.

Cleo dialed the next number and this time the man promptly hung up on her. "I guess Alice and Archie aren't working there either," she said, "but how rude to just hang up."

Finally on the seventh call, the girls got what they were looking for. "I gave the Cobbs explicit directions this morning when they called to confirm," said the woman.

Cleo waved frantically at Robbi, then pointed to the phone receiver. Her brain was working overtime to think of just the right thing to say. She couldn't afford to have this person hang up on her.

"Yes," said Undercover Cleo, "they asked me to call again. They're in the midst of moving and lost the scrap of paper with the directions. If you'd be so kind . . ."

The woman repeated directions to her house and when Cleo finally hung up, she triumphantly held the paper aloft. "Eighty-seventh Street right off Fifth!" she crowed. "They'll be there at ten tomorrow."

The girls joined hands for a quick, arm-splaying victory dance, then sank to the middle of the floor in a fit of laughter. Cleo lay on her back, looking up at the five dark chandeliers on the ceiling, and suddenly realized that she had neither the concentration nor the energy to make the drive home. On top of that, there was the unpleasant notion of having to drive at night.

She turned over on her side to look at her friend. "Rob, what would you think about staying here and going back tomorrow?"

"If you hadn't suggested it," said Robbi, "I would have." She picked up the phone and dialed home to tell her father she was spending the night at Cleo's house. With the Olivers away for the night, it was the perfect alibi.

The girls walked over to the huge windows that overlooked the ocean. The moonbeams were dancing on the rippling sea and the sky was a dark crystalline blue. In the distance Cleo and Robbi could see lights burning in the neighboring homes.

"I'm dying to turn on those chandeliers, but I guess we shouldn't," said Cleo.

"Definitely not," said Robbi, shaking her head. "Talk about your major tip-off. If we can see some of those other homes, you know they'll be able to see us." She sighed. "What *I'm* dying for right now is a Big Bart's Special." The Pizza Palace deluxe pie was slathered over with everything, even anchovies that Robbi adored, and the finished product probably weighed as much as the girl herself.

They had to settle for their homemade sandwiches in the dark, but both girls thought they'd never tasted such good peanut butter and jelly. They'd opened the cookies on the way to Southampton and now quickly polished off the package.

It was the ultimate setting for ghost stories and soon the girls were rehashing tales they hadn't told in years. After an hour they had succeeded in working one another into a thoroughly scary mood, especially after Cleo brought up a story she'd read about the Montauk Indians.

The town of Montauk was on the tip of Long Island, not too far from where the girls were now, and around three hundred years ago a powerful tribe of Indians known as the Montauks had lived there. One night the tribe was preparing for the wedding ceremony of the chief's daughter when they were attacked by a rival tribe. The Montauks were taken completely by surprise because their enemies had paddled across the sound from Connecticut by the light of the full moon. Many Montauks were killed and the chief's daughter was taken away by the enemy tribe, not to be returned for many years.

"They say on nights like this," whispered Cleo, "when the moon is out, you can sometimes still see the canoes gliding across the water." She shone her flashlight up from under her chin, making herself as frightening as she could. "You can also hear the war cries of the Montauk Indians echoing off the hills as they are being attacked."

"Enough!" cried Robbi. "Lucky for you we're not in Montauk or I'd make you drive us back right now!"

Cleo had forgotten just how much her friend was into the supernatural. "Okay," she said, laughing. "Come on, we should probably get some sleep."

The girls chose one of the guest rooms that overlooked the grounds and tucked themselves into a pair of twin beds. It wasn't long before Cleo heard the heavy breathing of her friend, but she had a hard time falling asleep and got up to look out the window one more time.

Something's wrong, she realized. *Alice and Archie Cobb might be the dognappers, but they couldn't have done everything themselves. Someone had to have told them about Mr. Edsel-Mellon's plans for the party on* Natalie's Dream, *and someone had to know all the details of the midtown office party.* She realized that if Undercover Cleo was going to do a thorough job, she had at least one more culprit to locate—the Cobbs' contact, probably someone inside the Edsel-Mellon household.

It was getting cold and the girl hurried back to the bed and snuggled under the covers. She drifted off to sleep wondering if Pepper Charvet's dislike of Bilbo was enough of a motive to mastermind a dognapping.

Chapter 28

The girls woke as the sun poked its fingers into the Edsel-Mellon guest room. They stretched and even toyed with the idea of sleeping an hour more, but knowing they had a chance to connect with the Cobbs made them anxious. They were also more than a little nervous about the possibility of coming face-to-face with a decorator or group of workmen, even though it was Sunday.

They snuck out of the house, locked the door behind them, and headed across the grounds. Cleo and Robbi took a last longing look at the entrance to the secret garden, then scurried over pebble paths to the beach.

Twenty minutes later the girls were on the Long Island Expressway on their way back to the city.

Robbi, who now considered herself navigator extraordinaire, read road signs, maps, and Cleo's scrawlings and got the girls safely to 57th Street. They parked the car in the garage and, greatly relieved to be rid of the gargantuan machine, took two buses to get to the house where the Cobbs were going to be working.

When they turned onto 87th Street, the first thing they saw was the battered gray van.

"Of course," said Cleo. "Now I understand the reason for the weekend work."

Robbi looked at her friend quizzically. "English, please," she said.

"The reason people in the city look for weekend gardeners and the reason the Cobbs went after that kind of job is parking," said Cleo. Because her father parked on the city streets, Cleo knew the New York City parking rules about as well as she knew her own phone number. "There's no street cleaning on Saturdays and Sundays and you can park anywhere. If you have to bring in lawn mowers and stuff, well, the weekend is the perfect time."

The girls strolled casually past the vehicle, then looked for the house where the Cobbs were working. Halfway down the block, Cleo and Robbi found themselves in front of a beautiful brownstone. The earth in the tiny flower beds in the front had been turned and white impatiens had just been planted, but the gardeners were nowhere in sight.

"If we could get a look into that backyard, we'd know if Alice and Archie are the ones we're looking for," said Robbi.

"Can't we peek over the fence?" suggested Cleo.

"What fence?" asked Robbi. The houses and apartment buildings were side by side on this particular Manhattan block with their walls touching. There wasn't enough space between the brownstones to slip in a knife blade.

The teen detective pointed to a beautiful building next door to the brownstone. The Frickenheim Museum had its entrance on Fifth Avenue and Cleo yanked her friend in that direction. "Time for some culture," she said.

The museum had once been the private home of one of the great robber barons, but it now housed a very exclusive collection of modern art. Devoted to American artists, the museum was also a popular site for benefits and cocktail parties. Cleo had been here on several occasions with her parents and Uncle Lionel and she knew that some of the exhibits were outside on the Frickenheim grounds.

The girls had to wait for half an hour until the museum opened, and Cleo was glad to see that among the people standing in line was a young family with several children under the age of seven. The teen detective hoped they would prove to be a distraction for the guards.

Cleo and Robbi followed the family through the museum at a comfortable distance and were pleased when they finally heard the mother tell the kids that they were headed outside to the courtyard. The girls could see the children were getting restless, which worked well for their plan.

The impeccably groomed museum grounds were filled with large sculptures in several mediums from marble to iron to wood and one of the great attractions of the garden was that visitors were encouraged to touch the artwork. Cleo knew it would only be a matter of seconds before the rambunctious brood was all over the pieces.

The guard had exactly the same thought and moved quickly to a rounded marble statue that the children were trying to crawl on. Cleo winked at Robbi and the girls worked their way to the stone and stucco wall that separated the museum grounds from the neighboring yard.

"Look, we're not going to have unlimited chances here," said Cleo, "so you'd better ID these people fast."

Robbi nodded and pulled the snapshots Cleo had taken at the bridge out of her pocket for one final glance. "Okay," she said, "ready for action."

The girls made sure the guard was busy watching the children, then stepped behind a clump of tall bushes near the wall. Quickly Cleo reached down, made a cradle with her hands, and gave her friend a boost up so she could see into the next yard.

Cleo watched as Robbi's eyes zeroed in, then her head started bobbing up and down excitedly. "Okay," she whispered. As soon as she was down she opened her mouth to speak, but before she got out a word a voice spoke.

"Hey! What are you girls doing?" The museum guard had arrived just in time to see Robbi jump down.

Both girls whirled to face the approaching man.

"Uh, sorry 'bout that, sir," said Robbi. "It's just that we're counting birds, you know, that Audible Society thing? It's like this contest at our school, and I was sure I saw this triple-breasted aqua-green woodpecker fly into that yard. It'd make fifteen kinds of birds for me, which would put me way out in the lead." She smiled proudly and stood up to her full four feet ten inches.

Cleo pressed her lips together and kept her eyes on the ground so she wouldn't start convulsions of laughter.

"Okay, okay," said the guard. "I understand, though I doubt you would have seen a woodpecker around here. Anyway, just stay on the paths here or I'll have to ask you two to leave."

"Thanks, sir," gushed Robbi. "We really appreciate this, and we promise we won't do it again. Just got a little carried away. By the way, this is a *great* museum. . . ."

Cleo dragged Robbi off in the midst of her babbling, and as soon as they were out of hearing range of the guard, the tall girl burst out laughing. " 'Audible Society'?" she said. "It's Audu*bon* Society." She collapsed in another fit of giggles.

Robbi didn't look that amused. "Well, whatever. At least we didn't get arrested. And," she said with a smirk, "it's them! I think we've got our dognappers."

That put a stop to Cleo's hysteria. "Okay," she said. "Now that we know that, we need to find out where they've taken Bilbo."

The girls left the museum, then walked across Fifth

Avenue where they sat on a bench facing 87th Street. It was unusually warm and it felt great just to be in the sun relaxing. Cleo and Robbi also knew that at any second they might be off on the next leg of their mission—following Alice and Archie Cobb.

"You know, I just realized something," said Robbi. "If they live far, like in Brooklyn or something, a cab ride could put us in serious financial trouble."

Cleo wrinkled her brow as she realized the truth of Robbi's statement. "Amira's" harrowing taxi ride earlier in the week had taught her how quickly a cab meter could add up, but how else could they follow the two suspects except by good old-fashioned New York City medallion cab? Without knowing a destination in advance, neither a subway nor a bus were feasible choices.

Then Cleo remembered how she'd spent nearly all her allowance on this latest caper and she slumped down on the bench. There was no way she had enough money to get across town, let alone take a wallet-busting trip to another borough. She looked up to see Archie Cobb carry a weed whacker out of the brownstone. He walked to the back of the van, opened the door, then exchanged the whacker for a leaf blower and a pair of hedge clippers. Cleo sat up straight in the bench seat as she watched the man slam the van door and return to the house.

"Hey," she said, pulling Robbi to her feet, "did you see that?"

"Yeah," said Robbi. "He's traded one air-polluting machine for another. So what?"

"No," said Cleo, a glimmer of hope growing as she moved toward the van. "He didn't use any keys to unlock the back."

She explained her idea to her friend and after making sure no one on the street was watching, Cleo reached for the van door. She pushed a button on the handle and wanted to shout when the door clicked open. Quickly the girls scrambled into the back of the vehicle. The growl of the leaf blower winding down let them know they only had a few minutes, and they wedged themselves in behind a huge lawn mower, then rearranged several leaf bags and the raking tools around themselves. All they could do now was pray that the pair of tired gardeners didn't notice them.

It wasn't long before the back doors opened once more and the girls held their breath as they heard tools being shoved inside. After the doors slammed shut again, the van's engine roared into life and the friends grabbed for each other's hands as the vehicle was put into gear and jerked forward.

Bumping along on the bare floor of a van was a far cry from the ride the girls had had in the Edsel-Mellons' gold Rolls-Royce. "How many potholes does New York have?" whispered Robbi after being heaved up off the floor for the umpteenth time.

"Two hundred fifty thousand?" said Cleo, remembering a statistic her father often quoted.

"Well, I'm sure we've hit at least half of them by now."

Cleo laughed, despite her own aching rump. The

girls had long since lost their bearings and were now simply holding on, hoping they'd never have to travel by this far-from-luxurious means again.

Just when they thought they couldn't take one more bump, they felt a blessedly motionless sensation. The van had miraculously reached its destination.

"Oh, no," they heard Alice say after the engine was turned off, "we forgot to buy dog food. Feel like taking a walk to the market?" Her voice was rough, almost manlike, and grated on the ear.

Cleo and Robbi each swallowed a gasp. That meant Bilbo was alive and close by.

"You gotta be kiddin'," said Archie. He had a nasally voice and spoke in sputtering sentences. "I'm exhausted. Forget about that dog. We'll be rid of him soon, one way or another." He opened the van door. "Come on, it's time for the Knicks game. They're playing Houston. You know, pretty soon, I'm not going to have to watch the games on TV anymore. I'm going to be right there on the floor with season tickets."

Alice grumbled, then opened the van door. "Yeah, well, don't pick out your seats yet, mister. If we don't get this over with soon, you may be watching from Riker's Island," she said, referring to the New York City jail. "Somebody's on to us. Remember that Indian girl from the party? Something was very fishy there. None of the undercover people at the party were supposed to be wearing a costume like that."

The girls heard the doors slam, let two minutes go

by, then picked their way out of their hiding place in the vehicle.

"Come on," Cleo said to Robbi. "We've got to see where they're going." She peeked out the van front window just in time to see Alice and Archie disappear into a brownstone halfway down the block.

The girls hurried out of the van to find they were in the midst of a cute neighborhood of brownstones and small apartment buildings. There was an overhead subway stop at the end of the block.

"Any clue where we are?" asked Robbi.

Cleo brushed herself off before answering. "Not the vaguest idea, but one thing I do know—we're not leaving without Bilbo."

Chapter 29

Cleo and Robbi went to the front door of the brownstone and into a small mud room area. Scanning the list of occupants, they saw the Cobbs' name on the ground-floor apartment. The door into the building proper was locked.

"How do we get them out of here?" Cleo asked herself. The teen detective bit her lower lip and stepped out to look at the house and its surroundings. When her gaze landed on a medium-sized apartment building next door, she smiled and slowly nodded. It just might work.

Entering the foyer of the apartment house, she told Robbi to push every buzzer on the wall. Moments later people were calling down on the intercom to ask who was there, but a few occupants just buzzed them in without even asking.

"What are we doing?" asked Robbi as they went through the front door. There was only so far she was willing to go without being informed.

"We're going to get into the Cobbs' place," said Cleo. "There's got to be a back door."

There was a door leading directly to the back, but Cleo first wanted to get a bird's-eye view, so the girls took a small elevator to the sixth and top floor and went out on the roof. They were glad to see the divider between yards was nothing more than a chicken wire fence. Among other things, Cleo noticed a rooftop exit on the Cobbs' building. It might come in handy.

Cleo and Robbi went back down to the first floor and out into the scruffy-looking backyard of the apartment house. As one girl lifted up the fence wire, the other slid beneath it into the Cobbs' yard. Just then a window opened, and they heard snatches of a loud conversation. Cautiously they crept toward the open screen.

"When are the Edsel-Mellons gonna be home?" asked Archie, obviously upset.

"Sometime in the afternoon, I guess," answered Alice. "They're probably back now."

"So, do you want to call?"

Alice sighed in exasperation. "We agreed on Monday, so we've got to wait until Monday or they'll think we're too anxious. Besides, the longer we wait, the more that little girl is going to nag her dad."

"Yeah. Either that or the whole bunch of them will just forget about the dog."

"She won't forget, believe me. That girl never let the dog out of her sight."

"Okay, we'll play it your way, 'Jeannette,'" said Archie with a laugh. "It's stuffy in here. I'm gonna open the door, let some air in."

Now how would Alice know that Lilliana took Bilbo everywhere? wondered Cleo. The comment, plus the earlier remark about knowing there would be undercover police at the midtown party, confirmed her theory about the Cobbs having a connection inside the Edsel-Mellon household. The question was, who?

Cleo shook her head. It was something she would have to sleuth out later. Right now she had a more important matter to attend to. She tapped Robbi on the shoulder and the girls crept away from the window.

"Look," she said, "wait here until you hear the phone ring. After they pick up, count to fifty, then start pounding on the door."

They froze as they heard Archie slide open the patio door that led to the garden.

Robbi stared at Cleo. "Hey, I'm not ready for the psycho ward yet, you know," she whispered. "How do I know those two aren't going to attack me with a weed whacker or something?"

Cleo shook her head vigorously. "No, no, no. Listen to me. I promise, you won't even see them. That is, if you . . ." and she whispered something into Robbi's ear. "But be sure to yell as soon as you start pounding."

Robbi grinned. "Just like on TV."

"Exactly," said Cleo. She and Robbi gave each

other a thumbs-up signal, then Cleo crept directly toward the Cobbs' patio door.

Robbi watched in horror as her friend peered in the small window, then quietly eased the patio door open. Cleo slipped inside, tiptoed into the room, and came back out in less than a minute. A moment later the tall girl crawled back under the fence and made her way through the apartment building next door. Out on the street she ran to a pay phone at the corner and quickly punched in the number she'd seen on the Cobbs' telephone just inside the back door. When Alice picked up, Undercover Cleo went to work.

Imitating Natalie's slight lisp, the teen detective said, "Hello, Alice? This is Mrs. Edsel-Mellon. I just want you to be aware that we know all about you and the police are on their way at this very moment. You're going to be very sorry you took Lilliana's dog." The girl hung up abruptly and raced back to the front door of the brownstone. At precisely the same moment that Robbi began to knock on the back door, Cleo pressed the buzzer to the ground-floor apartment.

Cleo kept her finger on the button and stuck her ear to the door when she heard Robbi yelling.

"Police! Open up! We've got you covered."

Cleo started banging on the foyer door and yelled as well, doing her very best imitation of Detective Milton's high voice. A second later she heard the front door to the downstairs apartment open, but instead of the Cobbs coming to let the police in, the sound of their footsteps told Cleo they were escaping up the stairs.

The teen detective smiled. This was exactly the move she'd anticipated the couple would make. As they escaped up to the roof, Cleo put two fingers in her mouth and let out a shrill whistle that was her coded message to Robbi.

The small teenager in the backyard ventured into the dingy apartment and when she saw the Cobbs were gone she hurried to the front door and let Cleo in.

"We've got to hurry," said Cleo. "If they realize there are no police cars around, they might be back."

That left the girls only seconds to find the missing Bilbo, and they ripped through every room in the apartment calling his name.

"He's not here," cried Robbi.

Cleo ran to the front door, locked it, then wedged a chair under the doorknob, hoping to buy a few more minutes. "He's got to be," she said. "Remember we heard them talking about dog food."

She forced herself to stand still and think rationally. Bilbo's picture had been published in every New York newspaper so the Cobbs wouldn't have wanted to risk the white puppy being seen. That was probably why they'd chosen to keep the dog out at Southampton. It had probably been a perfect spot until reconstruction began. Then the likelihood of someone hearing the puppy must have forced the Cobbs to bring Bilbo here.

"The basement," she said suddenly. No one would see or hear the dog if he was there.

The girls raced out to the hall toward the door to the cellar, and at the same time heard a clumping of footsteps coming down the stairs above them. In near panic, Cleo and Robbi bolted down the stairs into a dank and dimly lit basement and were rewarded immediately by a weak whimper coming from a far corner.

Bilbo, tied to a support post, was cowering under a moldy kitchen chair. The little puppy seemed to remember Cleo and looked up at her with the saddest eyes she had ever seen. Robbi untied the leash and after Cleo gave the dog a few reassuring pats on the head, she put him in her backpack.

"I hate to do this, Bilbo," she said, "but it'll be faster than letting you walk on your own."

Somewhere on the floor above them Archie began yelling, "What's going on here?" His voice was loud enough to rouse the whole neighborhood.

Robbi tugged her friend's sleeve. "Come on, come on. We're gonna be dead meat in a second."

The basement had a door that opened out into the backyard and in record time the girls had it open and were rolling under the fence. Soon they were brushing themselves off and hurrying through the lobby of the apartment building next door.

They were coming out the front entrance onto the street when Alice and Archie came puffing down the sidewalk toward them. Cleo felt her friend stiffen.

"They don't know who they're looking for," Cleo

whispered to Robbi. "Walk slow and act casual." As the two girls walked toward the Cobbs, Cleo prayed that Bilbo would stay quiet.

"Hey, wait a minute," said Archie to Alice, just as the girls went past. "You don't think . . ."

"What are you, crazy?" said Alice. "They're a couple of kids. Come on, maybe we can get in through the back." The Cobbs went into the apartment building the girls had come out of.

The girls stepped up their pace slightly as they headed toward the elevated platform. It was a stop on the E line and as soon as they saw the system map they realized they were in Queens. It wasn't until they were safely on the train car and headed back to the city that Cleo opened her backpack.

"Good dog, Bilbo," she said in soft tones.

The little puppy poked his head out and licked the girl's face, his eyes filled with gratitude and the understanding that he'd been rescued.

"I can't believe we actually found him," said Robbi. "You are truly amazing, Undercover Cleo."

Cleo beamed at the compliment, then turned serious. "I couldn't have done it without you," she said. "Thanks. We're not finished yet, though. Now we've got another problem."

"Oh, come on, give me a break, not another problem," said Robbi. "What are you talking about?"

"How do we get Bilbo back to Lilliana without ending up on the front page of Nortrud's tabloids?"

Chapter 30

Two hours later Cleo was sitting alone at one of the back booths of The Pizza Palace.

"Cleo," called a boisterous voice, "want to try one?" Big Bart held a large platter of small fried lumps, each skewered with a toothpick.

"Sure." The girl smiled and reached for what turned out to be a deep-fried, smoked mozzarella cheese ball. "Mmm, great, Bart," said Cleo. She bobbed her head up and down heartily. "They definitely get my vote."

Big Bart was always trying out new recipes on his customers and if he got enough positive response, the dish ended up on his menu.

"Everyone likes this one," said the big man, "so I hereby declare it a special for next week." He offered the girl one more, then moved off to the next table.

As Cleo was chewing the tasty tidbit, bells on the

door jangled and she looked up to see Lilliana coming in. Behind her, visible through the big front window, was Carl standing beside the parked limo.

"Lilliana," called Cleo. "Over here."

The little girl made her way through the crowded restaurant and took the seat opposite Cleo. "Hi," said Lilliana. "I'm so glad you called."

Cleo noticed there were dark circles under her friend's eyes. "Glad you could make it," she said. "I just haven't seen you in a while and I was wondering how things were going."

"Oh, okay, I guess," said Lilliana. "Daddy took us all to Disney World for the weekend. It was neat and everything, but it's kind of hard to have fun right now. I couldn't even sleep wondering when we'd hear from those people again."

The teen detective nodded sympathetically and looked over Lilliana's shoulder to see a tiny, older woman loaded down with a large shopping bag come waddling into The Pizza Palace.

"Got a menu?" asked the woman in a remarkably loud, obnoxious voice.

Cleo turned her face back to Lilliana, but kept one eye trained on the short lady who wore many layers of baggy clothing and a floppy hat. Someone behind the counter handed her a menu and she set her bag on the ground.

"Nah, tonight I think I'll have Chinese," said the woman. She looked straight to the back table, and from beneath the wide brim of her hat, Undercover Robbi winked at Cleo and then left the restaurant. In the hustle and bustle of the busy pizza parlor, no one except Cleo noticed that the shopping bag was still sitting on the floor by the take-out counter.

It took only two minutes until the bag tipped itself over and there was an outburst of oohs and ahs as several customers gathered around it.

"What's going on over there?" asked Cleo innocently.

Lilliana twisted in her seat and looked in the direction of the uproar. "I can't see a thing." She had just turned back around when she heard the bark of a small dog. "Bilbo?" she whispered.

The girl jumped out of the chair and jostled her way to the front of the restaurant where Big Bart was already pushing the rest of the people back. "Let's not scare the little fellow," he said.

Lilliana burst through the ring of customers who circled the puppy. "Bilbo!" The dog took a flying leap from the floor up into his young mistress's arms and the two went down together in a tumble of hugs.

By this time, Cleo had gotten up from the table to join the crowd of onlookers. There wasn't a dry eye in the Palace as everyone recognized Bilbo and realized who Lilliana was. It was at least a three-hankie moment. Even Carl, the surly chauffeur, who'd come in when he'd seen the ruckus, was smiling.

"Oh, Cleo, look," said Lilliana, "I thought I'd never see him again." She looked around the crowd, then turned to the teenager. "Okay, which one is your friend?"

The teen tried not to let her shock show. "What

friend?" She would have bet that Lilliana hadn't seen Robbi.

"The secret agent friend you said might help," said Lilliana. "I mean, I bet you talked her into finding Bilbo after all, right?"

Cleo played a moment of utter surprise. "Lilliana, I really meant it when I said my friend couldn't help. I have no idea how Bilbo got here." It was a performance worthy of an Academy Award.

The little girl wasn't sure what to believe, but she quickly shook off the thought and smiled. "Well, anyway, do you think you could come over for dinner? Please say yes."

At the moment all Cleo could think about was how tired she was. It had been an exhausting weekend and all she wanted to do was put up her feet and watch TV for a while, but she reminded herself the ordeal was not really over. The Cobbs were still on the loose and so was their inside connection in the Edsel-Mellon household. Until the dognappers were rounded up, Cleo wouldn't be convinced that Bilbo was safe. Dinner at Lilliana's would give the teen detective another chance to do some sleuthing.

Cleo sighed and smiled. "Sure, it'll be fun. I'll call home and ask if it's okay."

"Great," said Lilliana. "It'll be nice to have company for dinner."

"Everyone, look!" cried Lilliana. She ran into Mr. Edsel-Mellon's office where her parents were in a meeting with Elaine. Everyone was shocked, but

Cleo, who hung back in the doorway watching their reactions, thought they all seemed genuinely happy to see the little dog. Lilliana's father spoke first.

"That's wonderful," he said. "But how did you get him back? Darling, I hope you didn't put yourself in any danger."

Lilliana told the story of Bilbo appearing out of nowhere in The Pizza Palace. "He found his way to me, Daddy," she said.

The man nodded thoughtfully, and it was clear that he didn't quite believe such a thing was possible. "Well, it's a relief he's been found, anyway." He looked up into the doorway. "Who's your friend?"

"Oh, this is Cleo Oliver," said Lilliana.

Cleo entered the office and extended her hand. "Hi, we met at that party on *Natalie's Dream*. I was with my parents."

"Of course," said Mrs. Edsel-Mellon. "You're Scott Oliver's daughter." She winked at her husband. "I have a feeling your father will be very interested in a press release Mr. Edsel-Mellon will be making tomorrow."

Cleo crinkled her brow and tilted her head. "About what?" The woman's obvious glee was making her nervous.

Mr. Edsel-Mellon paused only a second. "I'll tell you what. I'll let you in on the news, and you can tell your dad tonight. It'll be a real old-fashioned news scoop." He took a deep breath before continuing. "Tomorrow we're announcing that my development plan for the West Side will include two public park areas, one to be called JP's and the other, which will include a petting zoo, will be called Lilliana's Place."

Cleo looked over to see the little girl was delighted and was giving her stepmother a heartfelt hug.

"Furthermore," said Mr. Edsel-Mellon, "we're not going to take away the Green Machine's planted plots. Natalie here has taken to gardening lately and she's convinced me how much everyone needs these patches of green."

Everyone looked pleased with the news and Cleo wished she could go home right away to tell her father. She was just wondering if it would be rude to ask if she could call him when the butler stuck his head in the door. "Excuse me, phone for you, Elaine," he said. "Your mother."

Elaine showed a momentary flash of anger, then regained her prim composure. "I'll take it in my office," she said, before turning to the Edsel-Mellons. "Don't forget your dinner engagement at the Russian Tea Room with Ms. Oscard."

The Edsel-Mellons nodded, said good-bye to the two girls, then hurried out of the office after the secretary.

Lilliana turned to Cleo with a huge smile on her face. "Wait here for a minute, okay?" she asked the teenager.

"Uh, sure," said Cleo. She watched as the girl raced out of the office.

Cleo wandered the room, then suddenly remembered the news she had to tell her father. She went to the desk and picked up the receiver. A gruff woman's voice was on the line. ". . . the dog's gone."

Cleo quickly hung up, embarrassed at having eavesdropped. But the words echoed in her mind, and she realized the speaker had been talking about Bilbo and not only that, it struck her that the voice had sounded very familiar. Cleo sat up in shock. Of course, it was the raspy voice of Alice Cobb, and she had called to talk to Elaine, which meant that the secretary had to be the inside connection.

Cleo didn't dare pick up the phone again, but she was dying to know what Alice had to say to Elaine. Her eyes darted around the big office until they landed on the brass sconce.

Thank you, Pepper, she thought as she hurried to the wall and turned the brass knob. The oak panel slid back and the teen detective vanished into the secret passageway that led to the secretary's office. The girl crept in as close as she dared, not trusting herself even to breathe.

"I don't know who brought the mutt back," said Elaine, "but you'd better not go back to the apartment. I'm sure whoever was pounding on your door has already tipped off the police. A hotel? Good, give me the number and address. I can't get away tonight, but I've got a break tomorrow around four-thirty. I'll see you then."

Cleo heard the tear of a sheet of paper, then the sound of the receiver being put down. The girl hurried back to Mr. Edsel-Mellon's office and closed the secret doorway, just before Lilliana came in the room.

To her surprise, the little girl carried two white dogs. Cleo didn't bother to mask her bewilderment as she waited for Lilliana to explain.

"This one's Bilbo, as you know," said the girl, "and this little girl doesn't have a name yet. She's the one those people gave Daddy on the bridge and Natalie said I could keep her, well, as company for Bilbo. I was sort of hoping you'd help me name her."

"Oh, wow," said Cleo. "That's so great that you're keeping her. Um, let me think. What's she like?" She watched as the little puppy scampered around the rug. It felt really nice to be asked to help with something so personal.

"I'm not too sure yet," admitted Lilliana. "She was pretty shy when she first got here, but every day she gets a little braver."

Cleo smiled. She knew the feeling well. She fingered the little silver charm on her belt loop, then looked up at Lilliana. "Hey, I know this is going to sound weird, but what about Butterfly?"

"Butterfly and Bilbo," said Lilliana. "I like it. Hey, Butterfly." She cooed at the puppy, who seemed to know her name already.

Cleo reached down and unclipped the safety pin that held the charm. Maybe she didn't need the reminder of who and what she was becoming anymore. Undercover Cleo felt like she had full-fledged wings right now.

"I had this to remind me of . . . well," said Cleo, "it's not important. Anyway, would you like it?

Maybe you could put it on Butterfly's collar, like a name tag or something."

Lilliana reached for the teeny silver butterfly. "I love it," she cried. "Oh, Cleo, thank you so much." She pinned it on the puppy's new collar. "Now she'll know who she is."

The girls played with the dogs until they were called in to dinner by the butler. Cleo stood up to follow Lilliana, but was careful to leave her pack on the floor by Mr. Edsel-Mellon's desk. Just when they reached the dining room, she "remembered" it.

"Oh, listen," said Cleo, "my pack's in the office. I'll just be a minute." Before anyone could say a word, she zipped off and down the hall.

It only took a second to grab her backpack, but on the way to the dining room she peeked into Elaine's office. Empty. Quickly the teen detective slipped into the room and scanned the desk for any clues. Spying a pad of notepaper, she noticed the lower half of the top sheet had been ripped off. Smiling, the girl reached out and took off the second layer of paper and stuck it into a side pocket of her backpack. Then she returned to the dining room.

It was hard to sit still through dinner, though Cleo had to admit that she even enjoyed JP's company. He was a bit of a geek, but it was definitely interesting when he talked about the on-line computer stuff he was into and the odd groups that congregated in that electronic netherworld.

"There are boards on everything," he stated. "I mean, I've even seen them for iguana owners."

Cleo and Lilliana laughed. It was hard to imagine people who kept iguanas as pets getting together on their computers and talking.

"What about lop-eared rabbits?" she asked half jokingly.

"I'm sure there's a group that talks about them, too," said JP. "Tell you what. When I find them, I'll download everything they've got and bring it to school for you."

Cleo couldn't believe that this was the same snooty boy who had come to Walton two weeks ago. "Thanks," she said.

"No problem," said JP. "There's all sorts of stuff you can learn on-line. If only I could use it to find out what happened to that Indian girl." He looked at Lilliana. "Did you know that Dad called up the Gutapundis? It turns out the whole family was in London at the time of the party. I don't even know who that girl was, but it wasn't their daughter." He sighed and shook his head sadly. "Talk about a total mystery."

Cleo took this as her cue to leave. It might be a mystery, but certainly not one that Undercover Cleo would ever solve.

Carl drove her home, and Cleo was so close to exhaustion that she fell asleep before they had gone two blocks. The chauffeur woke her up when they reached the Central Park West apartment and made sure the groggy teen got safely into the lobby. *I guess the nov-*

elty of riding in a limo's worn off, she thought sleepily.

She was only half awake when the elevator opened at the fifteenth floor, but managed to get inside and greet her parents, who were relaxing after their weekend of flea marketing. The teenager gave her father the news about the Edsel-Mellon project before stumbling to her bedroom and crawling into the comfort of her Chinese wedding bed.

It wasn't until the middle of the night that she remembered the slip of paper. Cleo sat straight up, pulled from her dreams by the knowledge that a potentially vital clue was tucked away in the side pocket of her backpack.

The girl clicked on her bedside lamp, retrieved the scrap of paper, then sat at her desk. Taking a soft pencil she rubbed it back and forth over the paper. Slowly an outline took shape of the depression made when Elaine had written down the phone number and address of a hotel on Tenth Avenue.

Time to bring in Detective Milton.

Chapter 31

"No way," exclaimed Robbi. "After all we've been through, we just can't sit back and wait. You're telling me that Sasquatch is going to get all the glory again and we won't even be there to see it?" Robbi had a way of giving people appropriate nicknames and this latest one for the large detective made Cleo giggle.

It was lunch period at Walton and Cleo had just given Robbi a lowdown on everything that had happened the night before at the Edsel-Mellon home.

"What are you saying?" asked Cleo teasingly. "That you want to be there to watch the arrests or something?" She'd already made up her own mind that she was going to be at the hotel for whatever went down.

"What else?" said Robbi. "Don't tell me you don't . . ." She stopped when she saw the look on her friend's face. "Okay, you got me that time."

"I'm sorry," said Cleo with a laugh. "I couldn't help myself. But look, I haven't even called Detective Milton yet. I want to make sure the Cobbs and Elaine are actually going to be there before I tip off the police. So if you're up for it this afternoon, we're on."

Robbi was so "up for it," she looked as if she were going to burst out of her seat right then and there.

The hotel was in an area of Manhattan with the dubious title of Hell's Kitchen. The girls left immediately after school and rode the M-104 bus down Broadway to 49th Street. From there they walked to Tenth Avenue where a fairly ordinary six-story hotel stood on the west side of the street—The Kitchen Inn.

Cleo headed for a large parking lot next to the hotel and looked through the wire fencing. "See if you can spot the van," she instructed her friend. They walked clear around the lot and were disappointed not to find the gray vehicle anywhere. "Maybe they're not here yet."

"Maybe they are," said Robbi, nudging Cleo and pointing. Parked at a meter near a side entrance of The Kitchen Inn was the battered van. "It's easier to make a getaway if you're parked on the street. I saw it on TV once."

Cleo nodded. Sometimes Robbi surprised her by saying things that made sense. In fact . . . The teen detective looked at the van, walked over to it, and smiled broadly when she noticed the small triangular window on the driver's side was slightly ajar. The girl pushed on one corner of the window until it was open at a perpendicular angle. Then, glad for once to have extra long arms, she reached in and pulled a black handle. The hood popped open.

Less than a minute later, Cleo was sure she'd cut off that avenue of escape for the Cobbs. "Come on," she told her friend. "Time to call in the troops."

Moments after an "anonymous tipster" phoned the 21st Precinct, the girls went into the hotel restaurant. At that odd hour they had the place pretty much to themselves and chose a booth at a corner window where they could see not only the entrance to the hotel, but the Cobbs' truck. They ordered sodas and sat back to wait for the show to begin.

It wasn't long before a dark sedan drove up and double-parked across the street. Todd Milton and his partner jumped out of the car and walked toward the hotel. The girls watched as the officers went to the front desk and began to question a clerk.

"Battle stations!" whispered Robbi.

Cleo merely nodded and took another sip of her root beer. She had mixed feelings. The case was coming to an end, which was a relief, but she also knew she had really enjoyed Undercover Cleo's adventures. She was going to miss her alter ego.

Two blurred shapes passing in front of the restaurant window shook Cleo out of her reverie. Alice and Archie Cobb had come quickly out of the side entrance and were racing across the street toward the gray van.

The two jumped into their vehicle, but to their surprise and dismay, it wouldn't start. Cleo and Robbi glanced at the hotel lobby, but the police officers still had their backs to the street.

"Great," cried Robbi, "Sasquatch is snoring over there."

Cleo jumped up and hurried into the lobby. Being careful to face away from Detective Milton and his partner, she pointed to the street and shouted as loudly as she could, "Someone's stealing that van!"

The two officers turned, their eyes going in the direction of Cleo's outstretched arm. They looked down at the photos in their hands and recognized the van that had been on the George Washington Bridge. The detectives rushed past the teenager, arriving at the stalled vehicle just as Mr. Cobb was lifting the hood to see what was wrong.

Cleo met Robbi at the cashier to pay their check and before the detectives had the Cobbs in handcuffs, the two friends were on their way out of the hotel. They walked down the block and casually leaned up against another parked car, watching as the Cobbs were put into the back of the police sedan.

"What did you do to that truck?" Robbi asked Cleo.

The teen detective opened her hand. In her palm was a pink fuse, just like the one she watched her dad pull out of the family car every time he parked it on the street.

Robbi laughed and high-fived her friend, then suddenly her eyes widened. "Get ready for part two," she said, pointing across the street to the hotel entrance.

A yellow cab had just pulled up and Elaine was stepping out. In a flash, Detective Milton and his partner jumped out of their car, arrested the secretary, and put her in the back seat with the Cobbs.

"Well," said Cleo, "I guess that's it."

Chapter 32

At home Cleo went into the TV room and flicked on the evening news. She was rewarded with a quick blurb on the arrests and a promise of a more extensive story at eleven. The girl groaned, knowing it would be hard for her to stay awake that late. She still hadn't caught up on the sleep she'd lost over the weekend.

A loud yawn came from the direction of her dad's office and she heard the creak of his chair as he stood up. These were the sounds of Scott Oliver taking a break so Cleo turned off the television.

"Hey," she said, peering into her dad's office.

"Hay? That's what horses eat," he answered, chuckling at his own awful joke.

Cleo had heard this one about a billion times. "Da-ad," she complained. She watched as her father picked up a couple of weights from the floor and did a few reps. "Finished for the night?"

"No, only taking a short procrastination," said Mr. Oliver. "Got an article due by midnight." He puffed and squinted, then let out a loud groan as he finished his burst of exercise. "Thanks to that scoop you gave me, I pitched an idea to the *Times* and they bought it. I'm doing a three-part series on the unlikely partnership of Herbert Edsel-Mellon and the Green Machine. How big-time development can coexist with a small grass roots organization and everyone will benefit. I met with both sides today, looked over Herb's plans, and I think it'll fly."

"That's great news, Dad," said Cleo. She opened her mouth to ask him how he and her mom had done bargain hunting when Mr. Oliver got a glazed look in his eyes. Without a word he walked back to his desk and sat down so abruptly that it seemed his knees had buckled underneath him, and began typing.

The girl sighed, knowing her dad had just been struck by a perfect sentence or perhaps an ideal structure for his three articles. Whatever it was, he was gone, no longer available for communication with any member of the human race. Cleo quietly exited and went to her room. If she was lucky, she could get her math homework done before dinner.

Phoebe woke Cleo the next morning. The rabbit had jumped on the bed and had positioned her twitching nose directly under the girl's nostril.

"Oh, Feeb," said Cleo. She stroked the bunny, then

suddenly remembered the eleven o'clock news. "Oh, no." She must have fallen asleep, even though she'd only meant to close her eyes for a few minutes.

The girl rolled out of bed and rapidly got dressed. The story had to be in the morning paper and she was dying to read it.

"Morning," she said to Nortrud. The woman was standing over the stove, stirring a pot of oatmeal, totally engrossed in a tabloid newspaper spread out on the kitchen counter.

"Morning to you, too," said Nortrud, her eyes never leaving the paper. "Would you look at this? Nice little article about that classmate of yours."

Cleo looked over the woman's shoulder and felt her eyes pop. The headline, JP'S MYSTERY CINDERELLA, was under a fuzzy photo taken at the office party showing Undercover Cleo as "Amira" talking to the boy.

The teenager was in shock because she hadn't noticed anyone taking photos of her. The article told of how the Edsel-Mellon boy had fallen in love with an exotic Indian "princess" and had even begged his father to hire a detective to find her.

"That's silly," Cleo said finally. "JP's only eleven."

"Well, I say it's sweet anyway," said Nortrud. "I wonder who she is? She looks a bit familiar, doesn't she?" The housekeeper reached over to turn off the heat and, without so much as a glance away from her tabloid, poured three bowls of cereal and put them on a tray.

"I'll take that for you, Nortrud," said Cleo, relieved to see the housekeeper turn the page of her paper. The girl picked up the breakfast tray and carried it into the dining room where her parents were having coffee. "I'll trade oatmeal for the Metro section," Cleo announced.

Mrs. Oliver smiled. "You've got a deal," she said, handing her daughter the newspaper.

Cleo sat and glanced through the headlines in anticipation. The dognapping story was a small column on page five, but it told her everything she wanted to know.

Everyone had confessed. The funny thing was, Elaine had done so in hopes of getting a lighter sentence for her parents and Alice and Archie Cobb had talked just so they could clear their daughter's name.

Cleo forgot all about breakfast and read on. It was definitely a bizarre story. The Cobbs had learned that their employer of many years was going to sell the Southampton estate where they worked so they had asked Elaine if the Edsel-Mellons might be interested in buying the property. Alice and Archie loved the gardens, and were positive this would be the perfect way to insure their continued employment.

Since Herbert and Natalie Edsel-Mellon were in the market for a beach home, it wasn't hard for Elaine to steer them toward the fabulous estate. She also made sure that realtors' messages concerning other properties got lost or their calls weren't returned. It didn't take long for the Edsel-Mellons to be convinced that this was the estate for them.

Unfortunately, the plan had backfired when Mrs. Edsel-Mellon said she wanted to hire a completely new staff. Elaine and Natalie had gotten into a bitter argument over the decision, but Natalie had insisted on having her way.

The secretary was trapped. She couldn't ask Natalie to make an exception and keep her parents on staff because then the Edsel-Mellons might figure out that she had manipulated them into buying the estate. Furious with Natalie and upset that her plans had been thwarted, Elaine had come up with the plan of taking Bilbo.

The secretary had convinced her mother to join the Green Machine, and the night of the yacht party Elaine had stayed in contact with her mother via walkie-talkie. After coming on board with the protesters, Alice had snuck away from the group and disguised herself as an elderly guest using clothing and a cane hidden on board by her daughter. The moment Elaine saw Lilliana and Cleo at the dinner buffet without Bilbo, she had radioed her mother and given her a location and the go-ahead to grab the dog.

Cleo smiled. Her dad had been right when he had told her not to look for just the obvious. It had turned out to be anything but, costing her every cent of four weeks of her allowance, not to mention the time and effort she'd put in.

Was it worth it? she asked herself.

Then Cleo remembered Lilliana's face at The Pizza Palace when she had recognized Bilbo's bark, and the sight of Lilliana kneeling on the floor hugging her dog.

Yeah, it was worth it.

She wasn't sure anybody would ever need her help again, but if they did, Undercover Cleo would be ready.